ALPHA DECEIVED

WAKING THE DRAGONS: BOOK 3

SUSI HAWKE

PIPER SCOTT

SANA

*P*eter wouldn't stop looking at me. I tried not to notice the way he sneaked glances in my direction and kept my eyes on the window, watching as the scenery outside the van passed us by. In the back seat, Sam was sleeping and Blaze kept a protective arm over him, shooing away our new puppies with his foot. I listened to the commotion and did my best to distract myself, but it was no use.

Every thought I had led back to Peter—the man who shared my heartsong.

I didn't want to admit that our hearts were connected. Being involved with anyone was more work than it was worth. I was a dragon warrior, and my life was pledged to defending the royal family. Full stop. It didn't matter that Peter made my heart feel like it was alive again. I couldn't afford to let him ruin my life's work.

We arrived at the estate after what felt like a decade spent on the road. I abandoned the car and hurried inside, leaving the others to get Sam, Blaze, the newborn twins, and the puppies settled. I needed some time alone to clear my head and get myself back under control. The soles of my shoes struck the wooden floors, and I tried to focus on the rhythm as my mind wandered. I'd been months without wasteweed, and my body was starting to recover. If I didn't find an alternative soon...

A force stopped me and spun me around, and before I had time to react, I'd already hit the wall. Breath catching in my throat, I looked up to find Peter looming over me. One of his hands pinned me to the wall by the shoulder. The other was braced at his side, ready to deflect an attack. We were both warriors, and he knew to expect me to retaliate by instinct alone. It was a damned good thing that he'd done this to me while in our estate—if he'd tried it anywhere else, he'd be in bloody pieces on the floor after that little stunt.

"Do you mind explaining what that music in my heart is? Because I know you're lying, Sana. You know what the fuck is going on, and you're going to tell me before it gets any worse."

It wasn't just his arm putting pressure on me anymore—he'd leaned into me with his full body, not bothering to hide the fact that he was rock hard. The breath in my throat retreated back into my lungs, and I closed my eyes and lifted my chin to expose my neck out of instinct. My heart hammered in response to his excitement, and it fired off treacherous signals in my head that made me want to submit.

"Or," Peter whispered. His lips brushed mine, and a jolt of pleasure shot through my core like I'd touched a live wire. "Am I going to have to fuck an explanation out of you?"

"You need to back the fuck off." It wasn't what I wanted to say, but I didn't have much choice. I lowered my chin and opened my eyes, combating my instincts. My chest rose and fell, and my lungs were squeezed so tightly with lust that I thought they might never be full again. "We can't do this here."

Peter glanced side to side, then pushed off my chest and left me standing against the wall. I'd been dodging questions like those for as long as I possibly could, but it seemed like there would be no avoiding them anymore. Peter wanted answers, and he wasn't going to stop until he got them from me.

"If you want to know what's going on, we need privacy. I won't budge on that." I pushed off the wall and rolled my shoulders back, working the dull pain of impact out of my muscles. Peter hadn't been gentle, and I didn't expect him to be. He was an alpha warrior, a man who'd served his kingdom —or country, I supposed—with his strength and capability. We weren't all that different, he and I.

Except for one little detail...

"You're afraid the other guys are going to see you?" Peter grinned, then glanced down at the sizable bulge behind the fly of my pants. I shifted my thigh to try to hide my erection, but it was of little use. These damned modern clothes left nothing to the imagination. "I guess it's not acceptable in your time for two alphas to be hot for each other? Because I don't give a damn. Alpha, omega, average human... it's all the same to me. Or is it the fact that I'm still not part of your group, and possibly one of the bad guys?"

"Can you shut your fucking mouth?" I asked, irritation prickling down my neck. I was glad Blaze had given me such thorough lessons in modern English, because I needed Peter to understand the severity of our situation. "Anyone could hear you."

As if on cue, one of the German Shepherd puppies our ever-growing family had just adopted skidded around the corner and rushed down the hall toward us. His tongue flopped out of his mouth, and the tips of his ears drooped down, bobbing with every hurried step. His tiny claws sought traction on the wood floor, then he launched himself at Peter's leg and snagged his pants with his teeth, tugging.

"Hey!" Peter said. He laughed and picked the puppy up. It should have been enough to break the moment and snap me out of my very dangerous want for him, but instead, it made me want him more. I eyed him as he tucked the puppy to his chest, and my paternal instincts went wild. Heat crept up my neck and flooded my groin. I'd never wanted someone so badly before.

If I didn't find some wasteweed soon...

Two other puppies scampered down the hall, distracting me. In the next moment, I saw what they'd been running from. A flustered-looking Emery appeared around the corner. "I'm so sorry, guys! They got into the twins' baby food, and I was trying to herd them into the bathroom so I could give them a bath, but they slipped out around my ankles."

"Here." Peter crouched down and scooped a second puppy up. The third growled playfully and took up his brother's post, nipping at Peter's pants. "I've got two. Sana, do you want to grab the last one?"

I didn't. In fact, I was already halfway down the hall in the opposite direction. Arousal had me wrapped around its little fingers, and I knew if I didn't get far away from its source that it would permanently twist me out of shape.

"Hey!" Peter shouted after me. "Don't think you can get away that easily!"

"Sana, are you okay?" Emery asked, confused.

I didn't reply to either of them. Instead, I stole down a corner and headed straight to my bedroom.

I had a hard-on the size of a fucking baseball bat to take care of, and I wasn't going to start taking care of it in the hall where anyone could see.

Peter wasn't just a dragon—he was the man who made my heart sing like no other. The one I wanted to stretch my neck to in submission in the hopes that he might claim me with his bite.

And that meant I was in shit so deep, I was never going to get out of it.

2

PETER

*H*e wasn't getting away from me that easily. I wrangled the puppies for Emery, made sure they were all locked in the bathroom, then took off down the hall. The music in my heart had stopped for now, but I knew it would be back. It had been plaguing me on and off since I'd met Sana, and I wasn't going to let it go unexplained anymore.

Something was going on here—something that had to do with the fact that Sana was a dragon. He wasn't going to leave me in the dark any longer. Fuck that. I deserved answers, and he was damned well going to give them to me.

I sped down the hallway, then rounded the corner. We'd only just arrived at the estate, and the layout was new to me, but a feeling in my chest led me right to where I wanted to go. When I approached Sana's room, I *knew* he was inside. It was like fishing line was wrapped around my spine, tugging me in his direction. The sweet melody in my heart grew more noticeable the closer I drew to the door.

No matter how much I wanted to storm the room, I was still a gentleman. I knocked. There was no answer.

"Sana?" I called out, speaking loudly enough that my voice would reach him. "Open up. We have something to discuss."

No answer.

Was he trying to test my patience? My temple twitched. What did he think he'd achieve by ignoring me? There was some seriously weird shit going on right now, and I needed to get to the bottom of it. If we were going to be working on the same team, he needed to be honest with me.

"I can *feel* you in there," I told him plainly. "If you don't open the door, I'm going to open it for you. We need to have a talk."

Nothing.

I drew an irritated breath through my nose and tried the handle. The door opened. With nothing keeping me from entering, I stepped into the room, ready to launch my investigation, only to stop short. Sana was on his bed, his fly open and his stiff cock in his hand. He pumped it urgently, his head thrown back and his neck on full display. His eyes were closed, and his jaw was clenched.

My cock throbbed, and I nudged the door closed with my foot and stepped forward. I knew I was invading Sana's privacy, and that I should have left as soon as I saw him touching himself, but he'd been turning me on just by existing since we'd met a handful of hours ago. Now that I saw him on the bed, spread out for me, I was like a dog presented with a steak —all I needed was his permission, and I'd devour him.

It was one hell of an effective way to get me to stop asking questions, I had to give him that.

I crossed the room, kicking off my shoes and socks on the way. By the time I reached the bedside, my hand was on the button of my fly, working it open. Sana lifted his head when my knee made a dip in the mattress. His eyelids were drooped, and his lips parted just slightly, like he wanted to speak, but no words ever came. I crossed the bed, holding his gaze, then sank down to his crotch and circled my tongue over the glossy head of his cock. He moaned for me, the sound way too primal to come from someone who presented himself as the definition of cool and collected.

"Fuck, you taste good," I whispered. I let my tongue circle his head again, dipping into his slit. There was no logical way he should have tasted as good as he did. I'd been with other alphas, and I knew what they tasted like. Sana was better than any of them, hands down.

He moaned again and threaded his fingers through my hair, holding me in place. I didn't mind. I *wanted* to be where I was, and I had no plans to stop teasing his cock.

"F-Fuck..." Sana arched his hips, pushing himself against my lips. I smirked, then kissed the ridge of his frenum. "Peter..."

"Yes?" I asked.

"I want your mouth. Let me breed your mouth," he panted.

"Not until I get some answers."

He still had me by the hair, so I couldn't sit back, but I wasn't going to take things any further than they'd already gone. My insane attraction to the handsome man before me made me want to give him my everything, but I knew that I'd never get answers that way. If Sana wanted my mouth, then he was going to have to give me what *I* wanted first. It was only fair.

Sana groaned. He pushed at the back of my head, trying to force me down onto his cock, but I was just as strong as he was. I resisted.

"Are you going to play nice, Sana?" I asked. "Because I can take this further if you want. I've been very kind so far, and

I've done my best to make sure all of you know that I'm not the enemy you might think I am... but if you don't tell me what's going on, I'm going to make you so fucking horny that you won't be able to stand it, and then I won't follow through."

"You're already doing that."

"This?" I chuckled. "This is nothing. Just *wait*."

Sana's fingers tightened, pulling my hair at the roots. I winced and lifted my head toward his hand, relieving some of the pressure.

"Suck me off now. I'll tell you later."

I hummed in disagreement. "It doesn't work that way. I need payment up-front."

"Fuck you."

"Not happening unless you tell me what I want to know." I arched a brow. "So spill. What's this music going on inside of me, and why does it feel like I've met you somewhere before?"

Sana winced, but his expression was softened by pleasure. He threw his head back again, baring his neck for me. A new, startling impulse swept through me, and I had to fight to hold myself back from acting on it. The sight of his neck stretched like that, his pale skin taut and exposed, made me want to sink my teeth into him so I could prove to the world that, beyond a shadow of a doubt, he was *mine*. My cock twitched, and I knew that a blowjob wasn't going to cut it anymore. Before I left this room, I needed to breed his ass and plant my seed in him. More than that, I wanted him to know that he'd been claimed—that I was there for him, and that he never had to worry again. It didn't matter that we were both alphas—my cock had never discriminated before.

His hand released my hair. I rose up, then tore his pants from his legs. Lean, muscular thighs led to sturdy calves. Dark hair curled at the base of his weeping cock, and I found myself wanting to bury my nose into it so I could suck his balls and nuzzle his length. He tasted sweet, and his scent was just as wonderful.

But it wasn't the hardened shaft vying to meet his stomach that I was most interested in. Tucked between his legs, currently hidden from view, was the hole I wanted to stretch and breed. We'd need lube.

Fuck.

"Tell me about the music I hear when I'm with you, Sana," I demanded. I cupped his balls and rolled them in my palm, and he moaned and stretched his neck farther. "What is it?"

"Th-The heartsong," he uttered. "That's the heartsong... what

ALPHA DECEIVED | 13

dragons hear when they've found a soul compatible with their own."

I rewarded him by tightening the pressure on his balls just slightly. He moaned and bucked into my hand, and it took all of my self-control not to pin him down and fuck him right there.

"Tell me more."

"You're... you're of draconian descent," Sana panted. "As... as I suspect every alpha and omega is."

I lowered my head and swirled my tongue over the head of his cock. He let out a desperate gasp that made my insides lurch with desire.

"And—" Sana's voice rose in pitch as pleasure consumed him. "—And you're meant to be my mate. We're meant to be together."

I didn't need to be convinced of that. My body was already highly attuned to him, despite the fact that we'd just met. I'd known from the moment I'd set eyes on him that I wanted to make him mine, but now I understood why. When I'd joined the Hunters' Guild, I'd been told about the existence of dragons, and I didn't doubt it for a second, based on the evidence they'd shown me. I'd never picked up on a single lie from those slimy bastards, so I knew that what they'd told me was true. My talent as a human lie detector had never led me wrong before... but as it turned out, it was useless for detecting second-hand lies—if someone truly believed that someone else's lie was true, it didn't set off my alarm bells. The underbosses I'd worked for in the Hunters' Guild had been right about the dragons, but they'd been so wrong about the threat they posed.

Dragons weren't trying to kill all humans and take over the world. All they wanted was a place to call their own. And the dragon I had in bed with me now? His needs were even simpler. All he wanted was to be fucked hard, and I was ready to give him everything he wanted.

"If we're meant to be together," I said huskily, "then I'm going to take what's mine."

I crawled up the bed, forcing one of my knees between his thighs. He parted his legs for me but didn't spread them. I had my hands braced on either side of his head, and I looked down into his stunning dark brown eyes. My cock begged me for his body. I needed him.

"Peter," Sana breathed.

"Yes?"

"You... you can't do this." His eyes were glossed over with lust. It only made him more beautiful. "You can't be so close to me, or I'm going to..."

"To what?"

I smelled it before Sana could answer, and a split second later, I knew exactly what it was that Sana was so desperate to hide. My eyes widened. Sana, the mighty alpha dragon warrior, wasn't an alpha at all.

He was an omega, and he was going into heat.

3

SANA

*N*eed spread like fire through my veins and swirled through my gut like fallen leaves caught in a breeze. I'd felt it coming on from the second that Peter had climbed onto the bed, invading my privacy when I was at my most intimate, and no matter how hard I'd tried, I couldn't keep it at bay. My heat ripped through me, leaving no part of me unaffected. I'd taken extensive, dangerous measures to make sure that I presented as an alpha, and it had been decades since I'd had my last heat... but Peter had undone all of my hard work in seconds, and I wasn't sure that I wanted what I'd lost back.

"You should have stayed away," I uttered. "I... I'm not what I seem to be."

"You're an omega," he gasped. The look of shock on his face

would have been laughable had my whole body not been in so much need.

"And you're the alpha who's meant for me." I bit the inside of my lip, trying to keep myself from giving my mind over to my impulses. "If you don't leave the room soon and get the hell out of here, my heat is going to consume us both, and we're going to..."

My cheeks heated. I imagined stripping Peter nude, his muscular body my present to unwrap. As each of his modern garments fell from his body, I'd see him like I'd never seen him before—a chiseled chest, a tapering waist, and best of all, a hardened cock ready to take my heat. I wanted it badly, and the longer Peter remained in my presence, the harder it was going to be to hold myself back. My dragon was already urging me to pin Peter down and work myself on his cock until he knotted my ass. It begged me to sink my teeth over his heart where our heartsong was the strongest to leave my mark on him, and offer him my neck so he could give me his mark in return.

The look in Peter's eyes told me that he wanted the same thing.

"Going to what?" Peter asked. There was mischief in his eyes. He grinned cockily and tilted his head to the side, claiming my lips in a sweet, heart-stopping kiss. I gasped into his mouth and kissed him back, but the kiss ended far too soon for my liking. "Make each other feel good?"

"You know what I mean. If you do this—if *we* do this—there will be consequences."

"Everything in life has consequences. Eat too much chocolate, you'll get fat. Work too often, you'll burn yourself out. Push yourself too hard physically, your body will give out on you... so what?"

"It's not like that," I uttered. I shifted my hips, already eager to have him push deep inside me. "I'm going into heat. You'll get me pregnant."

"Maybe that's exactly what I want."

What he'd said should have repulsed me, but instead, my heartbeat quickened and my cock throbbed. I parted my thighs for him, holding my hips up just a little higher. His body promised me relief from my heat, and I would do anything to get it.

Why hadn't I prioritized finding a source of wasteweed? All of this could have been averted if I'd only found some.

My attention snapped back to what was happening on the bed when Peter tugged the zipper of his fly down and brought out his thick cock. He pushed his pants down only far enough that his shaft was uninhibited—he kept the rest of his clothing on. Urgency built between us, equally as heavy in our heart-song as it was in the air. We didn't have time to strip each other—not when we needed each other so much.

"If you'd asked me a few months ago if I'd even consider taking a dragon to bed, I would have told you that you were fucking crazy," Peter said. He dipped his fingers between my legs and played with my shameful slick. I was wet for him and getting wetter by the second as my body urged me to mate. "But right now, Sana? Right now, the only thing I want to do is be inside you. I want to fill you up with my cock, knot you hard, and pump you full of my seed. I want to put a baby in that toned, muscular body of yours. I want to see you glowing as you swell with our child."

I don't think my cheeks could have been hotter—I'd held back dragonfire that didn't burn as badly as they did. I couldn't find the words to say, so I pressed down against his fingers as they explored my body. I wanted him inside me in the worst way, and I wanted him to know it.

Peter chuckled. He lifted one of my legs and tucked it over his shoulder, then replaced his fingers with the glossy head of his cock. He rubbed it through my slick, teasing my hole with every move of his hips. I moaned and rocked against him. I wanted that thick length inside me, pumping me full. It wasn't often that I let someone dominate me like this, and I craved the release.

"I'm not letting you leave this bed until you come for me," Peter told me. I was almost delirious with want, and I nodded my head in agreement. I couldn't hope to form words. "I don't care how many times that means I have to come in you, or how many times I have to pop my knot. I'm going to work an orgasm out of you, Sana. You're going to give it to me. Do you understand?"

"Y-Yes." My voice was hoarse, but I wasn't embarrassed. Peter had me too turned on to care.

My life as a warrior was in jeopardy, but something new was beginning—something my heat-addled brain wanted more than anything else. Before long, I was going to be a father.

Then Peter pushed into me, and all my thoughts bled away. I lost myself to lust.

4

PETER

*H*e was tight—almost too tight. I glided into him, but after the initial penetration, I had to take it slow. His body fit mine like a glove, and I was worried that if I pushed too far, too fast, that he'd tear. Even with his slick, he felt delicate. It was such an odd contrast, his hardened warrior body and his hidden omega features, but the dichotomy only made me want him more.

I liked his lips and the way they made the prettiest sounds for me. He was doing his best to stay quiet, but the hushed string of noises he made as I pushed into his tight ass couldn't be contained. A distant part of my mind wondered if he was doing it on purpose, or if it was an instinctual noise meant to get me horny as fuck so I'd want to mate with him.

"Fuck, Sana, you're tight." I wrapped my hand around his

cock and started to pump, working him toward orgasm. "Are you clenching for me? You don't have to. You feel so damned good."

"N-No," Sana managed to say. He rolled his hips, and I almost drowned in the sensation. I only realized after the fact that he'd done it because he was pressing into my hand, looking for more friction. I tightened my grip slightly and pumped him harder, hoping to give him what he wanted.

"Damn." I thrust deeper into him, unable to hold back. "A-Are you okay?"

"Yeah." As if to make a point, Sana curled up on himself and grabbed my hips, pushing me into him all the way in one abrupt movement. It knocked the air out of my lungs. "Go *harder*."

A switch flipped in my brain, and I let go of my inhibitions. Sana was an omega, sure, but he was a goddamn beast of a warrior, and a little rough play wasn't going to kill him. In fact, I had a feeling that the rougher we played, the better it would be for him.

I dropped his leg from my shoulder and leaned over his body, thrusting frantically to fill him up. When our bodies came together, the strange music in my chest amplified everything I felt, turning what should have been simple pleasure into a complex, rich feeling that made other partners dull in comparison. It was only our first time together, but I already knew that I was never going to want anyone but him ever again.

We bred savagely. His hips crashed against me to sink me in deeper while I pounded him. The bed shook. I was sure that someone had to be hearing us, but being discovered was the least of my worries. Right now, all I cared about was that the man my heart was drawn to was in need of me. I wouldn't let him down.

His tight body made it hard for me to keep going for long. My balls tightened, and my knot became harder to hold back. I lifted my head and met his gaze. "I'm going to knot you. I'm going to fucking knot you, Sana."

"I need it." His cheeks were flushed, and his body was glossy with sweat. "Put it in me, Peter. Make me *feel* it. I need to know what it's like to be claimed by my mate. I *need* you."

I let out a cry and pushed deep inside of him. My knot swelled, not in the slow way I was used to, but in a pulsing burst that shot fireworks off behind my eyes. I gushed into him, my cum more plentiful than it had ever been before. I worked my cock in shallow thrusts to push it deeper, nothing more than an animal at this point. Dragon? *Hell* yeah. I was a fucking alpha dragon who'd just discovered his purpose in life. I was going to breed my mate, and no one was going to stop me. I needed to make sure the world knew he was mine.

"Peter!" Sana gasped. His arms hooked around my neck and squeezed. I kept fucking him, pushing as deep as I could go. Our bodies were joined together, but that didn't stop me. I needed to work my seed deep. I needed to make sure what was mine was claimed. "Sh-Shit..."

I was still coming. How was it possible? My soul sang with Sana's, and my body acted of its own accord. I huffed out a breath and buried my nose against the crook of his neck, nuzzling and kissing. His pulse thrummed in time with our heartsong. I wanted to bite down and let the rhythm of his body wash through me, but I held back. Instead, I licked patterns across his skin and pumped my fist around his cock, encouraging him to come.

He gasped and pushed into my hand, and before I knew it, I felt him shooting. His cock pulsed, warm cum spilled, and his body tightened around my shaft. My hips kept moving, sinking into him in time with the rhythm of our heartsong.

"Peter!" he cried. "F-Fuck, Peter!"

"I'm going to do this again," I told him, never stopping. My hand slowed a little, but I didn't let it part from him, even as he slowly started to go soft. "I'm going to knot you all night long. I'm going to make you so full that you won't be able to move without feeling me inside of you."

Quiet tears streamed down his cheeks—happiness, not

sorrow. I could tell the difference, thanks to the bizarre new connection between us. It was going to take me some time to get used to feeling my mate's emotions. Hell, it was going to take me a while to get used to having a mate. I'd been alone my whole life, but it looked like that was about to change. I hadn't only found my long-lost brother when I'd crossed paths with Sammy again... through him, I'd found Sana—the man I was destined to spend my life with, and the man who was going to make me a father.

Pride swelled in my chest, and I let loose a hoarse laugh.

"What's funny?" Sana asked breathlessly. He was still moving his hips, sinking my cock as deeply into him as it would go.

I shook my head slowly. "I'm not alone anymore. I've found you. All the years I spent searching for something I couldn't put my finger on, and here you are... fuck. I can't believe it."

"Believe it." Sana drew my head down and kissed me. When the kiss broke, I was flustered. God, he pushed my buttons in all the best ways. "I'm real, this is real, and what we just did is real. You're taking my heat, Peter. You're going to make us fathers."

I smirked and kissed him again, hungry for the sweet taste of him. "Guess that means we should start getting to know each other better, doesn't it? I'll start. Hi, I'm Peter, and I'm going to love the fuck out of you and whatever babies you give me."

Sana's cheeks turned pink, just like I'd hoped they would.

"It's your turn, Sana. Time to introduce yourself."

He struggled for words. I saw the indecision pass through his eyes, and I felt his uncertainty hang in his soul. Then he shook his head and let his head fall back on the pillows.

"Hi," he said. "I'm Sana. And I've made a terrible mistake."

5

SANA

I closed my eyes, unable to look at the disappointment on Peter's face. It was bad enough I felt his emotions inside of me, an invisible force that I couldn't ignore. I knew that by speaking those words I'd hurt him, but the consequences of my actions were starting to tear me apart.

"You made a mistake?" Peter asked. His voice was soft and confused. He'd stopped thrusting, luckily, but his knot still tied us together. "What do you mean?"

"I shouldn't have done that." I kept my eyes closed, studying the patterns of light behind my eyelids. "I shouldn't have let you take me."

"Why?"

"You know why." I opened my eyes so I could glare at him, but before I could invest myself into the emotion, I gave up on it. The look on Peter's face wasn't just hurt—it was confused. He was built and stoic, but beneath his warrior's exterior, he was sweet and simple. I'd hurt him, and that hurt me. "You know what happens when you take an omega's heat... or are you going to be like Sam and deny that there is draconian blood in your veins?"

"I'm not going to deny it like Sammy did," he said. His gaze hardened. "I'm a human lie detector, Sana. I can tell that you're being truthful. Even if I hadn't tapped into my powers, I'd still believe you. After everything that's happened, and after everything I've seen? Why wouldn't I believe you?"

"Then why did you sleep with me?"

"Because my soul told me it was the right thing to do." He spoke with such an earnest quality to his voice that it was hard to hold what he'd done against him. I sighed and flopped back onto the bed, then hooked an arm over my face to cover my eyes.

It was my fault. Pinning the blame on him would get me nowhere. I'd been weak, I'd given into my heat, and now I had to deal with the consequences.

"Sana," Peter said. He continued to support his own weight, like he was afraid I might break if he rested on top of me.

"Can you tell me what's going on? Please? Because all of this is brand-new to me, and I have to admit that I'm confused as hell. I think I understand the heartsong, and I'm okay with the whole dragon thing... I'm even surprisingly okay that my soul has decided that I'm in love with a guy I've never met before. I'm under the impression that's all pretty standard dragon stuff, right? So why are you upset? I want to know so I can fix it."

I winced. "You can't fix it... not unless you can reverse time."

"I'm afraid I'm just a lie detector. I'm no time machine." He took my wrist and pried my arm away from my eyes, forcing me to look at him. I held back a sigh and met his gaze. He had stunning brown eyes flecked with reddish-amber, so close to brown it was unnoticeable unless I looked closely. I imagined he'd be beautiful in his dragon form. On every level, I was attracted to him... but I wished that we never would have mated. Now that we had, everything I'd struggled for so long to achieve would be taken from me. "You're upset that I'm getting you pregnant right now, aren't you?"

Saying that with his knot stuck up my ass was like a slap in the face. I grimaced.

Peter laughed. "Okay, I'm going to take that as a yes. Listen... I know you're from another time and all, and that back then you probably didn't have good reproductive health care, but you're in the modern world now. It's definitely not an ideal situation, but if you want, we can have the pregnancy terminated."

My blood ran cold. "What?"

"It's a thing. Sometimes, people get pregnant by accident. No one wants for it to happen, but—"

"No." My tone was icy. "That's not an option. No human medical doctor will touch my body. We need to keep our secret safe. All we want to do is live in peace—I won't have my king's secret aired in public because my fated mate triggered my heat."

"There's a pill you can take," Peter said. He lifted himself just enough so that he could strip off his shirt, and I was stunned to see that his skin was marked by designs—tattoos. They ran down his arms and across his chest between his collarbone and nipples. I was stunned by the detail in them. There had been tattoos in Novis, but the level of artistry and precision in Peter's tattoos was above any I'd seen before.

Between the pill he spoke of and the incredible tattoos on his body, I was reminded that I still had so much to learn about this strange new world.

"I do not trust human medicine to work on me," I said.

"It works fine on Emery... not that he's taken a morning after pill," Peter replied with a shrug. "I don't think your body is as different as you think. If getting pregnant is a problem for you, we could investigate it."

"No." My chest clenched. The dragon inside, usually silent, forbade me from considering it as a possibility. If Peter was to give me a child, I would have it.

We would have it.

There was no other choice.

"I don't know what I can do for you, then," Peter said. "I'm trying to help you. I don't see what the big deal is. Everyone else in your group is pairing off and starting a family... so why not you, too?"

Of course he wouldn't understand. He didn't know how I'd fought to get to where I was, or how well-guarded my secrets were. I shook my head slowly. "It's not the same for me."

"Would you care to explain why?"

"It's not the same for me because they don't know I'm an omega." I looked into his eyes, committing each amber fleck to memory. "To them, I'm an alpha warrior, just the same as they are. To them, I'm equally as strong, equally as capable, and equally as dominant."

Peter frowned. "Uh, well, I know we just met and all, but from what I've gathered, you *are* all those things. So what's the big deal?"

The generational gap and the cultural gap between us became obvious the longer I spent with Peter. He didn't understand how the world had worked when dragons were in power, and more than likely, he didn't understand what being an omega meant. I tried to find a way to make what I had to say succinct, but brevity wasn't an option when I had so much to fill him in on.

"An omega's function is to bear children," I said. "Their bodies are designed for childbirth. Physically, they are smaller and weaker than their alpha peers. Surely you know that much."

"Then why are you a walking wall of muscle?" Peter asked. "You don't fit that description at all."

"That's because I've worked my whole life *not* to fit that description. I've never wanted a quiet, simple life. Ever since I was young, I've worked tirelessly to erase the delicate, feeble traits that make me an omega... and I've succeeded until now."

Peter's knot was slowly deflating. I wormed my hips, hoping I could force it out of me, to no avail. We'd still be joined for a while.

"There are draconian heroes who are celebrated because they were brave enough to stand up for what they believed in, no matter their station in life. Lenis of Wynn was one such hero... an omega who took it upon himself to organize and prepare his settlement for battle as invaders approached on their location... but there is a difference between celebrated heroes and the reality of the world. Lenis was only in the settlement because omegas weren't allowed to enlist in the war efforts—only alphas are trusted in combat. If anyone were to find out that I'm an omega, I would be..."

"Be what?"

"Be ostracized," I murmured. "The truth is, Cory knows who I really am—he's my cousin, and he's been with me from the start. He wouldn't let me go if the truth were to surface."

"Then why are you so worried about it?"

"Because Brick and Blaze wouldn't tolerate it." It hurt to say things like that about my dearest friends, but I knew that it was true. If they found out I'd been lying to them all this time —that I'd been pretending to be something I wasn't—they wouldn't take it kindly. Even if they managed to get over my deception, they'd never treat me the same again. I knew that they'd step up in order to take over for the "weakest" member of their team, and they'd no longer trust me in battle. It didn't matter that I'd proved myself in combat time and time again, sometimes even besting them during practice—if they learned that I was actually an omega, they'd associate me with fragility, and I would never be able to convince them otherwise.

Peter picked up on my discomfort through the connection we shared. He wrapped me in his arms and hugged me close, putting his weight on me for the first time. The pressure was a comfort. I hugged him back.

"Then no one has to know," Peter said. "We'll hide our relationship, if that's what makes you feel better. If they figure out we're fucking, then we'll play it off as two alphas with the hots for each other. No one will have to know your secret."

I laughed bitterly. "Except that *everyone* will know, no matter how good you are at acting."

"What do you mean?"

"There's going to be a point in the future where it will become impossible to hide the fact that you've bred a baby into me," I told him flatly. "And even if I were able to conceal my pregnant body, there's the little problem that once I give birth, there's going to be a baby. I can't exactly hide that."

I felt his cock twitch inside me. His knot continued to deflate, but he wasn't going flaccid. Arousal sweetened our heartsong, and I felt it start to swirl inside of me again. He found the thought of knocking me up arousing, and that arousal swept through me and made me excited for it, too.

"Then what can we do?" Peter asked. "I've already cum inside you. More than likely, you're going to get pregnant."

"There is nothing we can do," I said. "What's done is done. The only thing I can do now is make sure I use what time I have left before my secret is revealed to make sure that the royal family is safe and settled. I need to make sure that I see to it that the Hunters' Guild is destroyed."

Peter had started to thrust again, shallow little motions that made me want more. I gasped and pushed my hips against him, trying to sink him deeper.

"It sounds to me like tonight is going to be a wash, then," Peter said. "Do you mind, since we don't have any other plans, if I stay in your room a little while longer?"

The panic and dread I'd felt upon realizing what I'd done was gone. Peter's desire for me drowned it out, and I rocked against him in total need. I'd never wanted someone so badly —the power of the heartsong was astounding.

"Stay," I told him, then kissed him savagely. When the kiss died, I whispered against his lips, "I've already made one terrible mistake tonight... what does it matter if I make some more?"

6

SANA

The next morning, we headed downstairs to breakfast together. My heat had subsided overnight, and I was still struggling to accept what that meant. The idea of pregnancy was a foreign concept to me. I'd always believed that I would serve Cory until the day I died, devoted to Novis and its royal family. The idea that I would find my heartsong had never registered, but here he was. I couldn't argue with the melody that filled my heart when he drew near any more than I could how a single touch of his hand had a way of making all my troubles seem insignificant.

I was in deep.

The grand dining room in the estate was lavishly decorated. Sam, Blaze's mate and Peter's brother, had been entrusted with spending our fortune in what ways he saw fit. He'd furnished the estate and found trustworthy men and women to maintain the premises in our absence. I approached the long oak table in the middle of the room and nodded to the others already sitting there. Embarrassingly enough, Peter and I were the last ones to arrive that morning. I was glad that Peter had volunteered to wait in my room for another handful of minutes so we didn't arrive together and arouse suspicion.

Too bad for us, it seemed like our cover had already been blown.

Blaze hooked an arm over the back of his chair and turned at the waist to give me a lingering look. There was mischief in his smile. "Good morning, Sana. You get any sleep?"

"I did, thank you." I sat in my chair and attempted to mind my own business, but Blaze wasn't done with me yet.

He smirked. "Really? Because I was pretty damned sure that I heard you fucking the night away. I didn't know you were into alpha-on-alpha action. All these years Brick and I have been barking up the wrong tree, haven't we? You don't want some soft omega to pump and dump—you want someone sturdy you can really wreck."

I wrinkled my nose. "I'm not wrecking anyone, Blaze."

Blaze rolled his eyes. "I mean with your dick. Wrecking someone with your dick, Sana. You know, giving them a good, proper fucking? The kind that knocks your headboard against the wall all night long and keeps me and Sam up?"

If it hadn't been for my extensive warrior training, my cheeks would have lit up like a bonfire. "Your suite is in the wing on the other end of the house from mine," I said.

Blaze gave me a pointed look. "Yeah. I know."

Peter picked that moment to stroll into the dining room. Every pair of eyes at the kitchen table rose to meet him, and he stopped in his tracks. The puppies, who'd been following him, fell over themselves as they skidded to a stop. One of them yelped and bit at his brother's paw, and a play-fight broke out.

"Hey, hey." Peter picked one of the puppies up and moved him aside. "No fighting."

"Making too much noise for you?" Blaze asked with a huge grin.

"I just didn't want them getting mean with each other," Peter said, lost as to Blaze's meaning. I covered my face with my hands. Emery snickered. "Uh? I think there's something I've missed?"

"Oh, nothing." Blaze waved his hand. "We're glad that you're able to walk this morning, that's all. Sana's always been so quiet and demure that we were all taking bets about what a freak he'd turn out to be between the sheets. It's always the quiet ones you've got to watch out for, right? I'm shocked you still have strength in your knees."

Peter's expression froze. I watched him lock down his emotions in an attempt to keep my secret, and I couldn't help but appreciate the lengths he was going to in order to respect my request. Despite the embarrassing situation, I found it inside of me to smile.

"I'm not sure what you're talking about," Peter said in a guarded tone. "I went to bed last night, just as I have every night. I think maybe you're thinking of someone else."

"Right." Blaze snorted. "Well, come join us at the table before your knees give out, man. We don't want to have to pick you up from a puddle on the floor."

I looked around the table, noticing everyone else's expressions. Brick, my unmated brother-at-arms, was looking Peter over carefully, as if he was assessing what kind of a man he was, and if he'd be a fair match for me. Emery, Cory's mate, was still snickering behind his hand while he tended to his daughter, Princess Cora. Cory, my king and cousin, was barely holding himself together—I saw his lips tremble as he suppressed a laugh. Sam, Blaze's peculiar little mate, looked distressed, as he so often did. He hugged his twins, Sophia and Tidus, closer to his chest.

So many small, happy families had been started since we'd come to the modern world, and I had a hard time accepting that soon, I'd be starting my own. The thought of having a baby to love appealed to me, but I didn't think I could ever be like Emery and Sam, who'd taken to fatherhood quickly and easily. I would always be a warrior—a baby wouldn't change that.

"I understand that there was some noise last night," I said in an attempt to diffuse the situation. "I don't know what you thought you heard, but I can assure you, there was nothing funny going on. Whatever it was must have been caused by something else."

"If you say so." Blaze looked like he was ready to start laughing, too. "I wonder what it could have been that made Peter moan your name loudly and repetitively at three in the morning while the headboard smacked the wall."

"Blaze, stand down," Cory said, even though there was laughter in his words. "We should be congratulating Sana for finally feeling comfortable enough with his body to bring a partner to bed—even if that partner is an alpha."

My gaze darted to meet Cory's. There was a sparkle of understanding in Cory's eyes, but he didn't give away my secret. I knew I could trust him. He would not betray me to the others. To do so would complicate our lives unnecessarily. For now, there would be peace.

"While breakfast is being served, we need to sit down and come up with a plan of attack for the next several months," Cory said. "There are several threads we need to tie up before we can rest. The rescue of the captive omega in the Alpine Compound, the whereabouts of our beloved adviser, Orris, and the destruction of the Hunters' Guild all need to be addressed. We'll need to figure out how to prioritize our time."

My stomach lurched with dread, and if I hadn't been sitting, I knew my knees would have gone weak. It was a lot of ground to cover in very little time. I had three to four months before my pregnancy started to show—perhaps a few more if I could find loose-fitting clothing. That didn't give us very long at all to get our missions over with before I was found out.

I had a few months to do years of work.

Great.

"Rescuing the trapped omega is our first priority," I said.

Blaze snickered. "It's not a trapped alpha, Sana. Are you sure you're still so interested?"

I shot Blaze a scalding look. Cory stepped in to put an end to the teasing. "Blaze, I believe I said that was enough. Sana deserves our respect."

Blaze mumbled something under his breath that made Sam elbow him in the ribs. Cora giggled.

I cleared my throat and ignored him. "Like I said, rescuing the trapped omega should be our first priority. We have no idea what the hunters will do to him if he's kept there for a prolonged time. In order to make sure he gets out safely, we need to take action. The rest will fall into place. Once we get him out, we can burn down the compound and weaken the hunters further. From there, I imagine it'll only be a matter of time until the guild disbands... or we exterminate them all."

"I agree with Sana's plan," Brick said. He sat a little straighter in his chair and looked at all of us. His salt-and-pepper hair and weather-worn face spoke of great wisdom. He was the oldest of all of us, and I always respected what he had to say. "Above all, we value life. If there is a trapped omega, it's up to us to set him free. The rest will come as it comes."

"But what of Orris?" Blaze asked. He crossed his arms on the table and leaned forward, looking Cory over. "He's been missing the longest. What if he's been captured? If he were free, he should have found us by now—especially since he took custody of the hoard in our absence. With money like that, he should be able to do almost anything."

Sam wiggled around in his chair uncomfortably. "Well, my security systems are top-notch. It would be very difficult for anyone to find this place, even if they had money at their disposal."

"Orris is a resourceful fucker, Sparky," Blaze said. "He's not human. The draconian blood in his veins and the extensive training he's been through as part of the royal family's entourage means that his skills should be sharp enough to find us if he wanted to. I would understand a few months, but according to Cory, it's been a long fucking time. So where the fuck is he?"

"If he was captured, I should have heard about it," Peter said. "If the Hunters' Guild had apprehended one of the evil dragons we were told would take over the world, every single one of us would have known about it. They would have flown us all in to the location he was captured so we could learn how best to kill something so dangerous. As far as I know, no dragon has ever officially been caught."

"Then there has to be something else keeping Orris from us," Brick said wisely. He met my gaze. "What do you think, Sana? Are there any paths we've left untraveled? Why is it that our adviser hasn't found his way to us by now?"

I shook my head. "I don't know. But the longer we sit here wondering, the more time we waste. We need to focus our energy on what we do know. Right now, there is an omega being held captive, and we need to make sure we get in there and free him before anything should happen to him."

"And maybe, while we're doing that, we can find out why he's been captured." Blaze rapped his knuckles on the table, then stretched his arms over his head and sarched his body from side to side. "Sounds like we have a plan, gentlemen. When are we going to get to it?"

"Tomorrow," I said. Everyone looked at me like I was crazy, but I knew there was no time to waste. My days left serving as a guardian to Cory were limited, and I was going to take advantage of each and every one of them. "Call Vivian and Nana. We'll need someone to look after the children while we get down to business."

7

PETER

"Sana! Hey, Sana!" Breakfast was over, and Sana was on his way upstairs. I caught him by the wrist seconds before he could climb the next step and tugged him around to face me. The others were busying themselves with preparations for our departure. It seemed like a waste to have left Vivian's so recently only to send everyone back there, but it was what it was. I understood the urgency in the situation better than any of them.

Sana clenched his fist and flexed the muscles in his arm, his body tightening as if to resist me. For a moment, I thought he'd spin around and punch me in the jaw, but when I saw his shoulders slump and heard him exhale slowly through his nose, I knew that nothing was going to happen. I had to remember that my mate was a dragon warrior, trained to always be on alert. If I wanted to keep all my bones in one piece, I was going to have to learn to approach him cautiously.

"You took me by surprise," Sana said evenly as he turned around to face me. I looked into his beautiful eyes and let the quiet strength in them wash me away. I wished he would let me behind his walls.

"I thought you'd know to anticipate me."

"Well, I didn't." Sana's face looked strained. "What do you want?"

I let go of his wrist, giving him some space. "I want to know what the hell that was about back there. Tomorrow? Don't you think that's a little soon?"

"No. Why?"

"Because we haven't even put together a plan beyond 'let's storm the castle.' If we're going to rescue the captive omega, we're going to need to go in with an idea of what we're doing. Our approach is going to need more finesse."

"Is the base really in a castle?" He scrunched his nose in confusion, and for a second, I forgot to be concerned.

I chuckled. "No. It's an expression. It means before we go rushing into some place. I know that you're not entirely used to this time period yet, but you have to trust me when I say that security is a lot more intense these days. People focus on keeping threats out rather than on how best to kill them when they come through their front door."

"Between Sam's technology and Cory's illusions, I see no point in worrying about detection."

"Well, as someone who used to work for those bastards, I do. We need to be more careful about this. I know that there's some urgency in our situation, but if we rush this, it's only going to make things worse. You can afford to spare a day or two."

Sana looked over his shoulder at the stairs, then nodded toward them. "We should speak privately."

"Yeah, I think we should."

"My room is closest," Sana said. "Is that okay with you?"

"Of course it is."

"Let's just go, okay?" Sana started up the stairs, clearly on edge.

"I wish I knew what was going on to make you so nervous," I said. "We still have time."

Sana looked back at me, pausing halfway up the stairs. "You will soon. Now come on, let's go."

BEHIND THE CLOSED door of Sana's bedroom, we had some semblance of privacy. To be honest, I wasn't sure that Sammy's gadgets weren't monitoring us full-time, but of all people, I trusted him to be discreet about personal information. I figured if Sana had a secret to share, this was the best place to do it.

"You want to know what I'm so nervous about?" Sana asked. He shook his head slowly, a worried look on his face. "I told you before—every single man in this building, apart from Cory, believes that I'm an alpha."

"So? They still think you are. I didn't say anything to give you away."

"Right now, my top priority is assuring the royal family's safety. That means that I have to make sure that the Hunters' Guild is stopped, and that Orris is recovered. That's a lot to do in the next four months."

"Why is it up to you?" I checked over my shoulder to make sure the door was closed. "Why is it that you can't have children when the other men who've sworn loyalty to Cory can? Blaze and Sammy have twins they're taking care of, and Cory hasn't asked Blaze to leave. What's going to change his mind about you?"

"How much time will I need to take for myself before the baby arrives?" he asked. The look of consternation on his face matched the anxiety I felt through our strange soul bond. "How much time will I need to take to recover after? Even if I give the child to you and let you care for it every hour of the day, the baby will still need me in his or her life."

"And?" I pinched my lips together. I didn't want to start a fight, but Sana wasn't giving me much of a choice. "You can say the same thing about Blaze and Cory. We've hit a rough spot right now, but it's not going to stay like that forever. Eventually, we'll all have time to settle down and care for our families the way they deserve. Until then, we need to keep fighting to make sure they stay safe."

"A job typically reserved for alphas." Sana frowned. "Do you know how much it will weigh on my conscience if I'm unable to fulfill my duties before I'm cast aside? I am one of Cory's last men-at-arms. If I'm forced to retire, or if I can't continue to satisfy my job requirements, then what? I've left my king without a guardsman in a time when he needs it most, and all because I couldn't keep my legs closed."

"Hey, hey, that's not fair." I held up a hand to stop him. "Your sexuality and your sexual choices shouldn't be used against you. Got that? I'm your heartsong. You met me, I pursued you relentlessly, and I triggered your heat. That's not something you chose."

"I could have told you to leave."

"You did." I looked at him flatly. "You told me to stop, but you changed your mind, and I wasn't going to argue. I should have listened to you the first time around. That's not your fault."

He said nothing, but the melancholy expression on his face, and the similar tug on my soul, told me that he didn't believe me.

I stepped forward, closing the space between us, and took his chin in my hand. I looked into his eyes and forced him to return my gaze. When I was sure he was paying attention, I spoke slowly but resolutely. "None of this is your fault. It takes two to make a baby, Sana. If I hadn't pushed you into sleeping with me, and if I hadn't been so relentless in pursuing you, none of this would have happened. You need to stop blaming yourself. I know that it's hard, and that when you're the outcast in a group, you put pressure on yourself that you otherwise wouldn't, but..." I trailed off, frowning. I remembered my own days as an outsider all too well. "Whatever happens? Whatever decisions your group makes? That's not on you. You're not the one who has to fix everything. You're supposed to be a team—Blaze and Brick need to step up, too. If they can't bring themselves to do it, that's not on you."

"Cory is my cousin," he stressed. "I need to make sure he's safe. I need to make sure that I keep the family protected. So I'm going to get this done quickly. They respect me for now, and they trust my word. The faster I mobilize us, the faster we'll get this done. We can plan while we're on the way. There's no doubt in my mind that between all of us, we'll be able to figure out what to do. But loitering here, where there are creature comforts? We'll grow soft and distracted. Movement means action, and even if we have to take a few days at our destination to figure out what we need to do, we'll be better focused there than we ever would be here."

He was a tactician, I realized—a sharp mind rounded out by a sensible tongue. Blaze, Brick, and Sana were all powerful dragon warriors, but it was Sana who possessed the wit to get them to where they needed to go. I wondered if Cory had brought him onto the team for that very purpose, but decided to distance myself from the thought. There was no point in getting caught up in the "what ifs." Right now, my sole focus was Sana and his comfort.

"If you're not going to listen to me, then let me listen to you," I said. I felt the turmoil poisoning our connection, and I wanted it gone. I was new to the whole fated mates thing, but I knew that I didn't want Sana to be upset. I wanted to get his mind off his troubles. "I want to know how you hid away all these years. Omegas in my time go through heats twice a year even without a partner. How did you keep the others from finding out?"

Sana snorted. He shook his head and looked at me. "If you

knew, you'd be upset."

"How?" I asked again.

"I poisoned myself." Sana glanced in my direction to check my reaction. I remained stoic. A handful of years in the military had hardened me to shock, and I didn't flinch easily. "There are certain plants that grew in abundance in Novis that I relied on to make sure I staved off my heat. Wasteweed, a common plant distilled to make a poison that weakens the body gradually, was my go-to. A small dose was enough to put my body under enough stress that my heats stopped. Over time, I learned to embrace how sick it made me feel."

"You'd rather poison yourself than expose who you really are?" I asked. I was starting to understand the severity of his secret. If he'd gone to such extreme lengths to make sure he was never found out, then he had to be genuinely worried about what would become of him. I slipped a hand around his waist and drew him close. "Sana..."

"Wasteweed doesn't exist anymore," he said softly, dodging my gaze. "Or if it does, it's changed to be unrecognizable. You don't have to worry about me poisoning myself anymore. I may not be proud of who I am, but I will not harm the child you've put in me. It deserves better than that."

I tugged him against my chest and held him close. My heart ached for him. "*You* deserve better than that."

"I don't. I don't deserve better than anyone else. We all do what we have to do in life."

"Poisoning yourself so you can live your dream isn't something you have to do in life."

"I chose to become a warrior, and I chose to take the steps necessary to achieve that position." He pulled back from me. Although there was sorrow in his eyes, I saw steadfast determination, too. Sana was stronger than I knew, both inside and out. "I could have walked away whenever I wanted, but I didn't. I saw it through. I got what I deserved."

He wouldn't let me win this argument. For now, I'd let him think that I'd given in. There was more than one way to convince a man otherwise, even if that man was a stubborn dragon who didn't want to hear what I had to say. "Alright."

"Is that it?" Sana chuckled. "All that resistance and you're just going to give up?"

"No one said anything about giving up. I'm saving my resources for when it matters. Right now, we've got to worry about renting cars and travel arrangements, don't we? The Alpine Compound is in Colorado. It's a hell of a long walk from here."

Sana laughed. "I think you've forgotten whose company you're in. We're not driving to Colorado, Peter... tomorrow, we fly."

8

SANA

"This," Sam said, voice tense as he snapped the strange armband to my upper arm, "is a silicone elastomer band with a storage pouch. It can stand up to three thousand percent elongation before it snaps. You're going to keep small, important things in it. Your IDs, mostly. If, god forbid, we get stopped by the police, you're going to want to have a few personal effects on you."

I looked at the armband. A pouch roughly the size of a pocket was sewn into the silicone band, and I felt various stiff plastic cards inside of it. There was a zipper at the top, making sure it stayed shut. Since I'd woken up in the modern world, I'd come to appreciate zippers. In some instances, they were much more convenient than buttons and pull strings.

My gaze wandered to Peter, who stood a short distance away,

and I sneaked a look at his crotch. Yes, zippers were definitely more convenient.

"Each pouch also contains a small object that will serve as a cloaking device." Sam tested the silicone band strapped to my arm by pulling it with his finger. Once he was satisfied, he unzipped my pouch and withdrew a device the size of a stamp. He flicked a switch on top of it, and a small white light blipped into existence. "Cory will take care of making us disappear when we hit the skies, but these little babies will make us disappear when it comes to detection technologies. Heat trackers, motion detectors, even something as simple as weather balloons tracking fluctuations in wind speed... we should be invisible to all of them. Scrambling isn't enough, because anyone with half a mind could follow the trail of broken electronics. As long as everyone has their devices on and in their pouches, it should be like we don't exist."

Sam put the device back in my pouch, then zipped it up. I looked from the pouch to him, seeking understanding in his eyes, but he'd already moved on to tend to Brick. Since he'd met Blaze, Sam had mellowed out a lot. I remembered the paranoid man he'd been when I'd first awakened from stasis, and was glad that he'd found solace in his heartsong.

I looked to Peter uneasily. The heartsong was supposed to be something wonderful, but it didn't always turn out that way. Sometimes, it caused just as much trouble as it did joy.

One by one, Sam activated the devices and made sure they were in each of the zippered pouches. When he was done, he tended to his own device and slid the armband into place on his upper arm. All of us except for Peter were shirtless—we'd kept our pants on while we waited for Sam to finish with his pre-travel briefing out of respect. Sam wasn't entirely comfortable approaching any of us naked, and Blaze definitely had a problem with seeing him anywhere near another naked man.

Peter, meanwhile, was wearing full protective clothing—a thick winter jacket, thermal gloves, thick thermal socks, boots, and long underwear to keep his legs warm. He looked bizarre standing in insulated clothing in the heat, but pretty soon, he was going to need all the warmth he could get.

"Cory, are you sure you're going to be okay keeping up an invisibility illusion around all us of for the duration of the flight?" Sam asked. He looked nervous, and he had every right to be. Yesterday, Blaze had given him a crash course in bringing out his dragon. They'd been working on it for a while, but today, he was going to put his skills to the test in one of the most extreme ways possible. "It's going to be at least ten hours, likely more, if the winds are against us. We need to make sure we stay safe for the loved ones we're leaving behind."

Cory's mate, Emery, was staying with his mother, Vivian, and

Sam's nana Gertie to help them take care of the children and the new puppies. They'd left earlier that morning with the bodyguards Sam had hired. Sam was reluctant to leave his babies behind, and although Blaze put on a brave face, I knew him well enough to see he was uncomfortable with the arrangement, too. The faster we got there, did our business, and got back, the better. Not just for me, but for everyone.

"I'm prepared," Cory said with a confident smile. "I may have been in stasis for thousands of years, but I haven't lost my edge. There were times I kept up my illusions for days to make sure we made it out of harrowing situations safely. This will be easy."

"You don't have to worry, Sparky. Cory is a fucking champion at what he does." Blaze hooked an arm around Sam's neck and pulled him close. Sam let out a little whoosh of air and closed his eyes, instantly calmed by Blaze's presence. "You don't know him like I do, but take my word that you'll never meet a finer dragon than Cory... apart from myself, of course. He's a royal for a reason."

"Right. Because I was born that way," Cory said flatly.

"No, because you'll give your everything to make sure those around you are safe and protected." Blaze grinned. "All of us can attest to that. Isn't that right, Sana?"

"Of course." I stepped forward, my shoulders proud and my

back straight. I beat my fist over my heart, a warrior's sign of fealty. "During our last flight, he must have gone close to eighteen hours without breaking the illusion."

"Not that it helped much," Cory admitted, his face falling. "But perhaps it's for the best. If we hadn't been attacked, we never would have been frozen for all those years, and Blaze and I never would have met our beloved heartsongs. I believe it's fate that we were frozen. The world we left behind was dying, and it's clear that the world we woke up in isn't... it just needs our help."

"No matter which world we're in, we will protect you dutifully," Brick said. He thumped his fist against his heart just like I had. "Are we ready to take off?"

"I'm ready." Cory nodded. "Everyone else?"

The rest of us nodded in agreement. Sam, who was the most reluctant, murmured something under his breath that made Blaze laugh and smack his back.

"You'll be fine, Sparky. You've been doing excellently until now. And you know what? If you get tired, then you can always transform back and let me carry you. I wouldn't mind."

Sam shot him a look that said he was in trouble, but it only made Blaze laugh more. It hurt to know that my closest friends had such wonderful relationships with their perfect matches—Cory with clumsy and sweet Emery, and Blaze with nervous and wickedly smart Sam—while my own perfect match had to be kept a secret. I rolled my shoulders back and shook the thought off. Negativity wasn't going to get me anywhere. I had a job to do, and once it was done, I could enjoy the bliss of my new connection. Until then, I had to keep my head in the game.

We stripped out of our pants. Peter collected them from us and folded them, slotting them into what Sam had called a hiker's pack. When he was done, he strapped it to his back and stepped out of the way. We were going to need space, and lots of it.

Cory, as our leader, was the first to embrace the transformation. I watched as he closed his eyes and accessed the flame in his soul. His body lurched and stretched, and before long, his skin started to give way to scales, and his bones and muscles began to reshape themselves to fit his new form. Around him, my brothers-at-arms had begun to shift, too. Blaze's beautiful blue scales glinted in the morning light, and Brick's stunning emerald-green color looked even more radiant than usual. As they transformed, I let myself go, too. The fire burned brightly in my soul, and it took no effort at all to stoke its flames and let it consume me whole.

Transformation seized my body, and I shifted.

My nose and jaw stretched. My neck grew both longer and

sturdier. My spine and ball-joints changed to accommodate my new quadrupedal body. My fingernails gave way to vicious claws. When my transformation was complete, I shook out my head and flapped my wings a few times to stretch them. The black and purple coloration in my scales didn't gleam as brightly as Blaze and Brick's jewel tones did, but I was fond of the way my amethyst highlights caught the eye. The black color of my scales denoted my rank as part of the royal family, even though my position meant very little. As Cory's cousin, I wasn't a recognized royal, and that suited me just fine. If I'd been more in the spotlight, everyone would have known I was an omega, and I never would have been able to live my dream.

Sam was the last one to transform. I watched him squeeze his eyes shut while he struggled to access the flame in his soul. While he was making tremendous progress, he still had a lot to learn before he was able to slip in and out of his dragon form without issue.

Blaze curled up on the ground beside him and stretched one of his wings to blanket Sam's shoulders. His touch was all it took—Sam's transformation began, and I watched in wonder as Blaze's curious little mate changed. His pretty teal scales glittered in the sunlight like gems. I wondered if he knew how beautiful he was.

Peter was the only one who didn't transform. He was

draconian—of that none of us had any doubt—but he was too new to his heritage to dream of accessing his wings, let alone his full dragon. He approached me, and I bent my neck down so he could climb onto it. His arms wrapped around my neck, and his thighs anchored him to me. I waited until he deployed the safety harnesses that Sam had come up with to make sure he didn't get knocked off, then lifted my neck again and craned my head from side to side, testing how secure the harness was. It didn't give, and Peter remained firmly in place. I was confident that nothing would happen to him during our lengthy flight to Colorado.

Cory beat his wings, stirring the air around us and scattering loose stones and grass clippings. Soon enough, his feet had left the ground, and he climbed higher and higher into the sky. His mighty wings beat down with great strength, granting him the force he needed to become airborne. The rest of us followed him, and I took up the rear, making sure that Sam managed to lift off the ground before I took flight.

My wings expanded, and I beat them down to get the force I needed to lift myself and Peter up. Peter's added weight made my job harder, but I knew once we were airborne, it wouldn't bother me much. The hardest part was separating my body from the ground.

When we shot upward, Peter let out a cry of delight. The sound filled my soul with joy, and I beat my wings harder to send us higher. Soon enough, we'd fallen in line with the other dragons, catching air currents to help us rise, until we were high enough up that we only had to glide. Cory directed us, and we all fell into line behind him.

It was like we were back in our own time again, the masters of the sky. I had to admit, it felt good.

We cut through the clouds and forged our path forward. A battle awaited us ahead—maybe my last as a dragon warrior. I would give it everything I had.

9

PETER

We landed as the sun set, touching down in a small section of secluded forest not far from a decrepit motel. With difficulty, I unhooked the harness that had kept me secured to Sana's neck, then climbed off him and laid on the ground. The tips of my fingers were frozen, and I was fairly certain my nose would never be warm again. We'd climbed high enough that the air had thinned and the temperatures had plummeted. Conditions like those in addition to the fact that we were traveling at high speeds meant that I'd just endured one hell of a frosty ride.

Sana shifted back into his human form and crouched over me. Our heartsong had made what should have been a torturous day easy. The music Sana's presence made in my heart allowed me to forget my suffering, and now that he was crouched over me, my numb fingers and cold nose barely registered. I smiled up at him, and he smiled with concern down at me.

"I'm going to make sure that whatever injuries you've suffered are taken care of," Sana said. He took my hand and stripped my glove off, then did something curious—he let one of his dragon claws sprout from his fingertips. It was tiny compared to what I was used to seeing from his full dragon form, but it was also wickedly sharp. He pierced my skin with his razor-sharp claw, then squeezed my finger until a fat bead of blood appeared. To my astonishment, he lowered his head and touched his tongue to my spilled blood.

The rest of the world melted away.

I closed my eyes and let relief wash through me. It was like Sana's spirit had invaded my body and wrapped my soul in an electric blanket. The numbness in my fingers faded into nothing, and bit by bit, he reversed the harm the cold had done to my body. When he was finished, I opened my eyes to find him looking down at me. His tongue had only been on my finger for a second, but his presence remained inside of me. It was a bizarre sensation, but I'd be lying if I said I didn't like it.

"You'll be fine," Sana told me in a comforting voice. "The injuries you sustained were easily reversed. I took care of them."

"You can do that?" I asked.

Sana chuckled. "Of course. My talents are linked to blood... healing is just part of my gift. Through a single droplet, I can detect and correct illness or injury, and I can also look back upon a dragon's lifetime or family history, tracing their blood-line for as far as I can stand. It's exhausting work, but it's something I love to do."

My respect for him grew. I'd been told that dragons were magical beings, but I hadn't realized how beneficial their powers could be. From the first day I'd been recruited by the Hunters' Guild, I'd been told that dragons only ever used their powers to destroy—but it was clear from Sana's talents alone that I'd been lied to. Dragons had the capacity to be dangerous creatures, but they were the same as any human— what they wanted was to live safe, happy lives. It turned my stomach to think that there'd been a time when I'd wanted them dead.

"Cory, as you know by now, has the power of illusion. Blaze learns through touch, and can look back through a person's memories or hear their thoughts. Sam can see waves and frequencies, and it imbues him with an understanding of elec-tronics unlike any other. Brick can manipulate the earth and force it to do his bidding... all of us have gifts. Even our missing adviser, Orris, has a power all his own."

It looked like Sana was getting ready to get up, so I set my hands on his bare thighs and kept him sitting on my abdomen. I didn't want him to go just yet, because I knew if he did, I'd lose the spectacular way he made me feel, so I stalled for time. "What can Orris do?"

"Orris can manipulate an object's relation to time," Sana said. "He can speed it up and make wood decay and rot in a matter of seconds, or he can reverse time's influence on an object and restore it to brand-new. He can only work with small segments at a time, and in sentient creatures, the change reverses quickly."

"Incredible."

"And then there's you," Sana murmured. He looked down at me with tremendous affection—affection he should be hiding, if he didn't want the others to know about us. "You can tell the truth by touching a person."

"Sometimes I don't even need to do that." I met his gaze, enchanted by him. I didn't think I'd ever met a man so perfect. "Sometimes I can tell if someone is lying just by looking in a person's eyes. Sometimes, even the tone of their voice is enough to tip me off."

"Your power is growing." Sana's smile grew. He pulled back from me and stood, then offered a hand. I accepted, and we rose together. The other dragons were transforming back as well, and it wasn't long before they'd clustered around me, looking for their clothes. Cory, Blaze, and Brick weren't shy about their nudity, but Sammy had gone to hide behind a tree. He peeped out from behind it every now and then, glowering.

"Sorry to break up the moment, but I've got to get my Sparky dressed. He's a little cranky when he's not covered up." Blaze unceremoniously dug through my hiker's pack while it was still strapped to my back. I widened my stance and braced my shoulders to try to keep it in place for him. Sana snickered as Blaze continued, "Goddamn, look at all this shit in here. What do we need all this stuff for? We're not putting on a fucking fashion show."

"It's important that we fit in, but it's also important that we have combat gear," Sammy called from behind the tree. "Plus, the four of you dragons are so beefy that your clothes take up extra space. It's not my fault that you're all built. If you were beanpoles, there wouldn't be half as much material."

"And we wouldn't stand half as much of a chance in a hand-to-hand fight, either." Blaze pulled out the clothing he wanted, then clapped me on the shoulder. "Thanks, pack mule."

"It's my pleasure," I said sarcastically.

When he was gone, Cory and Brick dug in. I rolled my eyes

and saw Sana hold back a laugh. I guessed, judging by his reaction, that this was standard behavior for his group.

"Make sure that you put on clothes you would normally wear out in public," Sammy insisted from behind his tree. Blaze had handed him his clothing, and he was in the process of getting dressed. "We're going to check into the motel over there so we can get our heads on straight about what we need to do next. The last thing we want is to attract attention."

I trusted Sammy. Our shared, troubled past had scarred him, but it hadn't kept him down. He'd grown into a cautious young man who planned for the worst, and that meant we'd never be caught with our pants down. I was glad to be back in his life and to be on his team.

"Then why the hell do we need to wear these unicorn shirts again?" Brick asked. I heard him shaking out a shirt from behind me. "Have we not suffered enough already?"

"We went over this already." Sammy sighed. "I suppose you don't know what a convention is. I can't blame you for that. Just... know that you won't stick out, okay?"

I'd only half-listened to their conversation about the best way to blend into the small part of Denver we'd landed in. A conversation about unicorns had devolved into some bitter jokes by the dragon warriors, and hearty laughter at Brick's expense over some private joke I wasn't in on. I didn't let it get to me. I knew that as their former enemy, I still had a lot to prove. If it weren't for Blaze and Sammy standing up for me, I never would have made it this far.

Cory and Brick finished collecting their clothes. When they were done, Sana helped me unstrap the pack from my back. He lifted it from my shoulders and set it down, then rooted through for his own clothing. Since everyone was busy getting dressed, I let myself watch Sana's ass. He was bent at the hips as he rifled through the pack, and the view was absolutely sublime.

Cory cleared his throat and slapped my back. I jerked my gaze away from Sana to look at him. He stood at my side dressed in a hot-pink shirt featuring a white unicorn with rainbow locks. The look on his face was telling. "Glad to see that you endured the flight. You did exceptionally well for someone who's never flown long-distance before."

"Do many people have the chance to ride on a dragon?"

Cory laughed. "No, which makes it even more incredible. With a little training, you could become a dragon warrior in your own right."

"Do you think so?" On the inside, I puffed out with pride.

"I know so. Your body is already hardened by combat and equipped for a fight. If you were to get in touch with your dragon, I could see you quickly becoming as skilled as any of my men-at-arms."

"Except for me," Blaze called from near Sam's tree. He was hopping around, trying to get his skinny jeans to fit him. It looked like he'd accidentally snagged Sam's—there was no way those pants were going up over his muscular thighs. "No one's as good as me."

"I don't know," Brick said, smirking. He tugged a neon-green shirt with a powder-blue unicorn down his chest. "I seem to recall a certain time when we were escorting Cory on a diplomacy mission to Lynnec where you were—"

"Oh, don't even start," Blaze warned with a laugh. "I'll fight fire with fire, unicorn boy. Try me."

It was good to see that Sammy had found himself such a loving group of friends. The banter between them made me feel welcome, even though I wasn't a part of it this time around. Someday, I hoped they'd accept me as one of their own... but with everything going on with Sana, I wasn't sure that would ever happen. Could men like Blaze and Brick really change their tune about Sana just because he was an omega? I thought about how protective Blaze was over Sammy, and how he so often stepped up to make sure he kept Sammy safe, and I wondered if my Sana would face a similar fate.

I was starting to understand why he was so nervous about the others finding out the truth. He wanted to be treated as an equal. Sammy, who was delicate and needed to feel secure, didn't mind stepping back to let Blaze take control, but I knew Sana would never be like that. He was a warrior through and through, and to deny him the freedom he wanted would crush him.

Eventually, everyone finished getting dressed. Sammy collected the zippered pouches and turned each of the little devices off, then returned them to my bag. While he did so, I stripped out of my thermal clothes and tucked them into the hiker's pack, then lifted it to my shoulders. I didn't bother strapping it on because we didn't have far to go. The motel was just beyond the trees.

"The rest of you are going to stay outside in a group while Peter and I go into the office," Sammy said.

"Why Peter?" Sana asked. I held back a smirk—there was a subtle hint of jealousy in his voice, and it turned me on like mad to think that Sana was puffing up his feathers for me.

"Because Peter is my brother-of-the-heart, and he's the one I trust out of all of you to act like a normal human being. It'll take us all of a few minutes to get our rooms booked. Until then, the rest of you will wait outside and stay out of trouble. You got that?"

"Stay out of trouble? With these fuckers?" Blaze laughed and kissed Sammy's temple. They were sweet together, and I was glad that my brother had found someone to love him so completely. "We'll try our best, but we can't make any promises, baby. We're trouble waiting to happen. You'll just have to hope nothing catches our eye while you're gone."

PETER

Sammy had things under control in the main office, just like I knew he would. I waited by his side, my hands tucked into my back pockets, while he haggled with the middle-aged woman behind the counter about room rates. While they went back and forth, I thought about Sana and the mission we were about to embark on together.

I'd been deployed and served time overseas. I'd been under fire, and been the one firing. I'd taken lives before. It wasn't something I tried to think about, but it was an unavoidable facet of who I was.

Regardless of my experience, I found myself terrified.

For the first time in my adult life, I had a family. Not only had I found my long-lost brother, Sammy, but I'd also met his mate, and the small group he was a part of. I'd met Sammy's nana Gertie, who'd adopted me on the spot and had promised never, *ever* to bake for me. But, most importantly, I'd met Sana—my mate.

I let that knowledge wash through me. I'd known all my life that something was strange about me, but until he'd come into the picture, I'd never put it together. Alphas and omegas were rare, and to be one of them... to know what it meant...

I'd met my heartsong, and we were going to have a child.

Going to war hadn't scared me half as much as the idea of raising a son or daughter did. I'd never cared about going into combat before because I'd always known that there would be no one around to miss me if I died. No one had ever depended on me. Now, in nine short months, I'd meet the life that would depend on me for the better part of two decades.

What if something happened to me?

Worse than that, what if something happened to Sana?

I looked over my shoulder out the window of the office. The dragon warriors and their king were crowded around the parking lot outside, talking and laughing. I caught a glimpse of Sana's face. He wore a polite smile, and he was laughing along with the others, but I could tell by his body language that he was uncomfortable. He was likely going through the same emotions I was. He hadn't been looking for me, and I couldn't help but feel like I'd thrown a wrench into his life.

I wanted nothing more than to make him happy and protect him, and one day into our relationship, I was already doing a shitty job of it.

I pinched my shoulders together and turned my gaze away from the window. More than anything, I needed to calm down and think. Emotions would only drag me down and keep me from making rational decisions. I needed to make sure that I approached this as logically as possible so I could take appropriate action.

"That's fine," Sammy said abruptly. He was in the middle of a conversation with the motel clerk. I'd missed most of what he'd said while thinking. "Please charge my card for two nights for each room."

The woman behind the desk took Sammy's credit card and narrowed her eyes, trying to focus on the name embossed on the bottom of the card. "I'll need to see your driver's license, Mr. Brown."

Sammy slid another card out of his wallet and presented it to her. She looked over the license, back at Sammy, then down at the license again. "Not often we have someone from Montana coming to visit."

"No, I suppose not." Sammy took his license back. He had

more fake identities than most people had clothing, and I had to wonder how he kept track of all of them. "We were hoping to keep going straight down into Texas before we stopped for the day, but we were too ambitious. It's a long, boring drive."

"I'd imagine." She slid the card through her processing machine, then handed it back to Sammy. "What are you boys up to in Texas?"

"Nothing," Sammy said. He tucked his card back into his wallet. "We're going past it into Mexico. Vacationing. We've got a boat down there, and we're going to set sail and forget about the rest of the world for a while."

"Sounds nice." She handed Sammy three envelopes that I assumed contained key cards. "I've heard you have to look out for ruffians in those parts."

Sammy gave her a look that was equal parts disbelieving and skeptical. "I don't know what world you've been living in, but you have to look for ruffians in *all* parts. The world isn't a safe place, you know. There's lots of danger out there. Lots."

He tucked the key cards into his pocket, turned, and marched toward the door. I followed along behind him, somewhat in awe that the shy Sammy I knew from my childhood could stand his own in a conversation. The bell above the door jingled, and we found ourselves back outside.

"Everything go okay, Sparky?" Blaze asked.

"Everything went fine." Sammy handed one of the envelopes to me, then the other to Cory. "We should be good for the evening. I have a few devices on me that should scramble any security equipment in the next five to ten minutes. It'll eat old recorded footage, so unless someone is glued to a monitor waiting for us, we should be good to go."

"Really? That's not like you, Sammy." I frowned. "You're overly cautious all the time. Why are you not concerned now?"

Sammy looked at me, a devious sparkle in his eyes. "Because I've already casually assessed the electronic frequencies going on in this place, and there's absolutely nothing that leads me to believe that anyone is watching. I haven't picked up on a single bug. Not a single one. Not even The Man is here, and that means we can rest easy tonight." He yawned. "And after a flight like that, I'm exhausted. Can we go over tomorrow's plans quickly so that we can all get some sleep? It's hard work, flying."

"We'll meet in my room," Cory said. "I'll be sharing it with Brick tonight, as long as that's fine with you, old friend."

Brick nodded. "It would be my honor."

Cory met my gaze for only a second, but it was long enough that I understood what his meaning was. In his own small, subtle way, he was giving me his blessing to be with Sana. I wished I could have thanked him, but with Sana insisting that we deny our relationship, there was nothing I could do.

Blaze slapped me on the back as he followed Cory in the direction of his room. "Looks like someone's going to get reamed by a certain dragon warrior again tonight, huh, dragon hunter?"

He smirked at me as he passed, but I said nothing. All I could do was hold back my laughter.

If only he knew.

ALL OF US gathered around the full bed in Cory's room. Sammy had produced a map, and he was in the process of smoothing it out on the sheets. Sana bent over to give it a closer look, his eyes narrowed. I watched him, wondering what was going on inside his head.

"We're looking for the Alpine Compound," Sammy said. He pointed at the topographical layout of the Rocky Mountains. "According to what Peter has told us, we're looking for a base approximately..." Sammy uncapped a fabric marker with his teeth and dabbed at the map. "Here."

I shook my head. "No. That's not it, Sammy." I took the marker from him and circled the location of the base on the map. "I know exactly where it is, and you know why? Because it's hidden on Sampson Peak."

Sammy looked up at me, startled, then shook his head and sighed. "Of fucking course."

"It's not like I chose where it was going to be. It was built before I was even part of the Hunters' Guild." I looked over the map and located the approximate position of the motel we were staying at. I circled it. "It's not far from here. I've never been to visit the Alpine Compound before, but it's my understanding that it's only accessible via helicopter. We're going to have to fly in."

"That's not a problem." Sana gestured at the map. "This is some kind of height measuring system, isn't it? There was a similar system in my time, and I think I'm starting to understand it. There are altitudes, aren't they?"

"They are," Sammy said.

"Then there's no problem. We've flown higher than this before." Sana bent over so he could trace each of the rings. "It will be hard work—we won't be able to drift in on an air current—but it's doable. With Cory and Sam there to cloak our presence, we won't have to worry about detection. All we need to worry about is landing."

"Not exactly." I knew better than that, and I was eager to finally prove my worth to the team. I pointed with the marker at the location of the base. "There are security measures in place, despite the fact that it's only accessible via helicopter. We're going to need to get Sammy somewhere he'll be able to shut down some of the interior security. Sammy, what do you need?"

Sammy snorted. "Not much. If I have access to an electrical panel outside the compound, that'll make my job easier, but if I need to, I can improvise."

"That's my Sparky." Blaze kissed the side of his head. "And I'm going to be your backup. Brick, are you comfortable protecting Cory?"

Brick bowed his head and pounded his fist to his chest. "It would be my honor."

"That leaves Sana and Peter, which I'm sure Sana will have no problems with." Blaze winked. "Seems like we've got some good teams set up. Do you think, with all of our forces combined, we can get the omega out and send the place up in flames? Or is this going to be a two-part mission?"

"It depends. We'll have to weigh our options when we get there." I let out a low, steady breath to ground myself and pulled together my thoughts. "There's heavy security. There will be trained personnel there that won't be happy to see us if they catch us. I have total faith that Sammy has invented something that will erase our signatures as far as any security devices are concerned, and that Cory can make us blend in so we're not detected by onlookers, but we need to be prepared for worst-case scenarios."

"There will be no worst-case scenarios," Brick said softly. He met my gaze, his eyes infinitely wise. "We have held our own for centuries, even through the worst."

"But if we get caught here—if all of you get hurt enough you submit to stasis—then there won't be anything to stop the hunters from killing you." I handed the marker back to Sammy, then looked in Sana's direction. There was an undercurrent of discomfort between us, and I knew exactly what it stemmed from. Neither of us wanted to face the very real fact that we might not make it out of this alive. "We need to prepare. We need to know exactly what we're doing if something goes wrong."

"We'll do what we always do," Cory said. His voice was firm, and it drew our conversation to a close. "We'll fight."

11

SANA

"*A*fter talking with everyone, I've had time to think about it, and... you need to sit this one out, Sana. I can't risk you like that."

"You're out of your mind."

I'd barely closed the door to our small, dingy rental room when Peter had turned on me. I looked him over, trying to figure out what had possessed him to suggest such a thing.

"What value are you adding to the party?" he asked.

"Excuse me?"

"If you're just coming as a bodyguard for me, then you shouldn't go. You can stay here and keep safe in the motel while we rescue the omega. I don't need a babysitter. I know what the hunters are capable of because I was one of them. I know exactly what to expect."

I thinned my lips. "I'd expect behavior like this from Blaze and Brick, Peter, but not from you. Who are you to tell me what I'm capable of? You barely know me."

Peter's face fell like my words had shattered his heart. It pained me to hurt my mate, but his behavior toward me was unjustified. I hadn't devoted my life to honing my physical strength and sharpening my combat abilities to be cast aside and deemed some soft, doe-eyed creature suited only for breeding. I was a warrior, and I would be until the day I died.

"I didn't mean to say that you aren't worthy, I mean that I don't want anything to happen to you. If it comes down to me getting hurt or you getting hurt, I'm going to be the one who takes the fucking bullet. We may not know each other well, but there's that damned heartsong in my chest driving me crazy, and there's a little life growing inside of you that we both need to make sure stays safe."

My heart wanted to shatter right along with his, but I held firm and refused to let it bog down my spirits. Peter had given me a gift that no other man had—a baby—but I didn't feel much like a father right now. We were still so close to my heat that I couldn't even detect the change pregnancy made within my own blood.

Peter frowned and shook his head slowly when I said nothing. "I didn't mean to say you're not capable, because you are. In a fight, me versus you, you would win, hands down. I won't deny it. I'm man enough to accept when I've been bested. But this is something different... this is something bigger than us. I know that we're new to this whole heartsong thing, and it's not something either of us were expecting, but now that we've bonded, we have a hell of a lot more to think about than ourselves."

I was silent. I couldn't find it in me to speak. Whether I wanted to admit it or not, there was truth in what Peter was saying. In nine months, we would be parents, and it was my duty to protect the life inside of me, just as I'd protected Cory for all these years.

"I'm sorry that it's like this, Sana." Peter frowned. "I'm sorry that life is tense right now, and that we're in the middle of a dangerous situation that's preventing us from getting to know each other, but... we need to consider all facets of this situation. We need to make sure that you and your friends are kept safe, but we also need to make sure that what we've made together doesn't come to harm." He stepped forward and laid his hand on my belly, stroking the tight skin there that would one day stretch as our dragonlet grew. "This is what matters to me, Sana. *You* are what matters to me. I know that we don't have a lot of shared history between us, but the heartsong tells me that I need to keep you safe. It won't let me do anything but."

"You're an alpha through and through," I murmured. I looked into his eyes and my heart skipped a beat. "Possessive of what's yours, protective to a fault, hard-headed..."

"I'm not that hard-headed," Peter said. His hand slipped from my stomach to my waist, and he tugged me close. Our chests met, and as the melody of my heartsong exploded inside of me, my arousal started to swell. I didn't want to be a slave to my body, but goddamn did Peter make me want to submit to him. "I *am* hard elsewhere, though."

"You're not the only one," I murmured. I wrapped my arms around his neck and ground our bodies together, rubbing my hardening cock against his. "Are you going to make good on your alpha status, then? Fuck me into submission until I'm a blathering, spineless shell of a man who'll always do your bidding? Is this your attempt to get me to stay at the motel while you 'storm the castle?'"

Peter smirked. "It's worth a shot, isn't it?"

"Good luck," I said with a hollow laugh. "You can fuck me all night long, but you're not going to make me change my mind. I'm not going to back down from my duties. I need to see this through, and if you want to come along and keep me safe, that's your prerogative—just stay the hell out of my way and let me do what I was trained to do."

Peter's eyes sparkled with mirth. "Are you saying you don't think I can keep up?"

"I'm saying that you can do what you want, but I know what I'm capable of, and I'm not going to let you keep me from doing it."

"So this right here, this little..." Peter bit his lip and set both his hands on my waist, grinding me against him with more urgency. "*Tease* that you're subjecting me to... it's to get me to change my mind, isn't it? To let you run amok into enemy territory regardless of the life we've made inside of you?"

"Maybe it is." I grinned at him. "Is it working?"

"About as well as you telling me that you're going to go ahead with your duties regardless of your safety."

Damn that man and his mouth. I couldn't get enough of him. We may have been strangers, but the banter between us was hot as hell, and I lost myself to it entirely.

"So if I have sex with you—if I let you knot me all night long —it's not going to make you forget? You'll still be determined not to let me do my job?"

"Absolutely." Peter leaned closer and let our lips brush. The taste of him was intoxicating—indisputably alpha. "But that doesn't mean I'm not going to have sex with you anyway. You can't tease me with something like that and then not follow through. How much sleep do you think you'll need for tomorrow?"

I grinned and kissed him hard, making the kiss my own. He moaned into my mouth and kissed back, and it wasn't long before we were stumbling across the room to sink down onto one of the two tiny beds. He boiled my blood and made me feel weak, but in the same breath, he made me want more than I'd ever wanted before. This was my mate—the man I shared my heartsong with, and who'd fathered a child inside me. My soul knew he was right for me. Now all I needed to do was convince my brain of the same.

"Less than you," I gloated as I straddled his hips. "Are you going to do your best to wear me out?"

"Damn straight I am."

He grabbed me by the shoulders and shoved me down against him. Before I had time to react, he'd already rolled me over and pushed me flat on the mattress. A breath parted from my lungs, and I looked up into his eyes to find them both aroused and playful.

"Are you trying to prove that you can best me?" I asked, amused. "Is that your game?"

"Is it working?"

"No." I smirked and grabbed both his arms, rolling us back. The bed was too small to wrestle with him the way I would have liked, so I had to make do. "But it is getting me fired up. What's on the line if I win?"

"My ass."

My smirk sharpened. I reached up to cup his cheek and tease him about losing, but as soon as I did, he grabbed my wrists, threw me off him, and pinned me to the bed. He secured my wrists above my head, holding me captive while he laid across my body and ground his hips down onto me. Pleasure bloomed in my groin, and I moaned and pressed up to meet his thrusts.

"Sana, you're so fucking hot," Peter whispered against my lips. I wanted to kiss him, but every time I lifted my head to try, he pulled back. "You're going to let me win, aren't you?"

"Why would I do that?" I loosened the tension in my arms and body, saving my strength for the moment I'd push him off me.

"Because you're not even trying anymore," Peter said with a wicked grin. "You're letting me hump you while you lie prone. You *want* this."

"Is it so bad to want something that gives so much pleasure?" Everything he was doing was turning me on—the way he moved his body, the words he spoke, and the cocky expression on his face. He thought he had me beat. "But if you're so insistent that I should deny myself, then..."

All at once, I thrashed my arms to the side and lifted my torso at the same time. Peter grunted in surprise, and while he struggled to regain his balance, I pushed him off me. He toppled from the bed and landed on the floor, and I landed on top of him. I grabbed both his arms and held them to his sides, then started to grind against his lap.

"Fuck, Sana!"

I grinned. "Not now. Soon, maybe... if I decide to let you."

"If this is your attempt at proving to me that you can take care of yourself... I get it."

"Good." I didn't stop grinding. My cock was at full mast now, and I wanted him. "Then I don't want to hear anything else about it. I have a job to do, and my pregnancy isn't going to take that away from me. I can handle myself."

"You know that I'm going to be there looking after you."

"You already said that. What I said before stands—don't get in my way."

His chest was rising and falling, but I saw the rebellion in his eyes. I braced for him to try to tug his arms out of my grip, but instead, he channeled his energy into flipping himself onto his side. I toppled from his lap and lost my grip only to find him on top of me, the hard outline of his cock flush against my ass. He nipped the ridge of my ear. His hot breath disturbed the short hairs on my nape. I closed my eyes and tried to resist the shiver that swept through me, but it was impossible.

"I'm going to fuck you so hard, you're not going to be able to move," Peter uttered. His hand darted between me and the floor, undoing the button of my pants. The zipper beneath gave, and he tugged the garment from my body. Then he lowered my boxer-briefs just enough that the elastic was caught beneath the curve of my ass. His bare cock traced along the valley of my ass, and I shivered again. "If you weren't pregnant before, I'm going to make you fucking pregnant now. I don't want there to be any doubt. If we're going to do this, we're going to do it right."

"Then what are you waiting for?" I asked. "Go ahead and take me, Peter. See how far you can get."

A primal growl rumbled in Peter's throat. It woke the omega in me and made me want to submit, but I pushed past my instinct to stay true to the man I really was. My heat was over, but I'd slicked myself for him, and he wasted no time pushing inside of me to claim what was his. I gasped and curled my fingers against my palm, overcome with pleasure. For a while, all he did was thrust lazily into me, tempting me.

"Does it feel good?" Peter asked. His voice was weighed down with arousal.

"Fuck yes, it does." I pushed back against him, then summoned all of my willpower and bucked my hips away from him. His cock slipped out of my body, and as he yelped in confusion, I rolled him over one more time. My slick spilled plentifully, and I dipped my hand into my own mess, pulled the front of my boxer-briefs down, and lubricated my length. "So good, in fact, that I think it's time that you understood just how wonderful it feels."

If he didn't think I could take care of myself, I'd prove him otherwise. I was every bit as powerful and dominant as he was, and it was time he learned it for himself.

12

PETER

Sana's cock felt a hell of a lot thicker pressed against my ass than it did when it was in my hand. I let out a startled breath and looked over my shoulder at him, turned on as hell. I'd had my fair share of sexual partners in my day, but never one who'd taken control like this.

He pushed inward, giving me ample time to refuse him if I didn't want it. He didn't need to take his time—I wanted it. I'd promised him my ass, and now he was going to take it.

He grunted as he pushed into me, invading my tight, virgin ring. I moaned and lifted my hips, trying to help him find a better angle. I knew that I was tight, and my nerves weren't helping. If he wasn't careful, he was going to split me in half. I already felt so full of him that I wasn't sure I could take any more, and he'd only just begun.

"You feel so good on my cock," Sana whispered against the back of my ear. I closed my eyes and moaned, doing my best to loosen for him. He pushed deeper into me, putting pressure on a spot inside of me that made me gasp and thrust back against him. He chuckled. "And I guess, if that was any indication, you think I feel good, too."

He thrust into me a few more times, hitting that spot with every rock of his hips. I braced my palms against the floor and pushed back against him, and soon enough, we were fucking in earnest. The sounds of our bodies working in tandem consumed the tiny room we were in, and I found myself hoping that the motel had thick walls. Blaze, Sammy, Cory, and Brick had to be hearing everything.

"How are you so tight?" he asked between clenched teeth. He hissed in pleasure and pushed into me a few more times, drowning out my common sense with pleasure. I moaned loudly—loud enough that Sana clamped a hand over my mouth and punished me by brutally thrusting into me. Tears of pleasure beaded in the corners of my eyes, and I trembled as I struggled to contain myself. I was going to come.

"Don't make a noise," Sana said. "You can't let them know that you're being fucked by a dragon warrior, can you? It would be embarrassing if they found out that I've got you pinned, and that you're helpless against me."

I wasn't helpless—I just didn't want this to end. I pushed

against Sana, eager for his body. My balls were tight. If he went just a little longer and just a little harder, I'd come.

"You don't want them to know that I'm going to shoot my seed inside you," Sana murmured. His words were meant to tease me, and they did a damned fine job of it. I moaned into Sana's palm. "When they find out the truth—when they know that I've been an omega all this time—what will they think when they learn that I pushed you to the ground and fucked you senseless?"

I didn't care what the hell anyone thought, because this felt too fucking good. I pushed back against Sana, craving more.

"I'm going to come inside you, Peter," he whispered to me. "I'm going to mark you from the inside. And one day, when I put my mate mark on you, all of them will see. All of them will know."

I sucked in a needy breath, seconds away from orgasm. Sana bucked into me a few more times, then stilled and pumped in shorter, far more shallow thrusts. I felt his seed rush into me, and I sank my teeth into his palm to bite back the cry that was building up inside.

"Oh fuck, Peter. *Fuck!*" Sana thrust a few more times, then stilled. He laid on top of me, depleted. "You're amazing."

I pulled my mouth away from his hand and knocked him off my back, then parted his legs and pulled his body up to me so

I could run my cock through his slick all over again. He moaned and arched his hips for me. His cock lay spent upon his stomach, and his cheeks were flushed.

"You are, too," I told him. Then, without warning, I thrust inside of him again.

It felt good to return to his warm, wet heat. I clenched my jaw and fucked him, working myself back up to the place of desperation I'd been in before he'd come inside me. A string of tiny noises tumbled from his lips, and they propelled me to go harder and faster. Even though he'd come, Sana was loving it.

And he'd love taking my knot even more.

My balls clenched, my body tightened, and I shot inside of him. As my orgasm arrived, my knot began to swell. In the next few seconds, we were locked together.

Sana let out a tiny, pleased moan and let his arms fall back onto the floor. I didn't imagine it was comfortable, but there wasn't much else we could do. I carefully lowered myself onto him and closed my eyes. Now that we were both spent, it was time to catch our breath and bring our pulses back to normal.

"Peter?" Sana asked lazily from beneath me.

"Mm?"

"I'm sorry that I've been prickly toward you. It's not you... it's the circumstance. That doesn't give me a right to be such a bastard, and you have my apologies."

"You don't need to apologize." I kissed his cheek. Our bodies were both hot and sweaty, and the floor was cool. I ran a hand through Sana's hair, clearing it back from his forehead. It was dark—almost black—and in certain lights, I thought I could see ultraviolet glimmer through it. It reminded me of his scales, and I had to wonder why it was that Sana's hair was like that when Blaze's and Brick's were what I'd consider to be a normal color. "I understand that things are tense, and I know what it's like to be under pressure. I was a warrior, too, once... but those days are over. I fight for myself now, and I protect those that are close to me. That doesn't mean that I've forgotten. I know where you're coming from... and I can only imagine how the heartsong and your pregnancy are making what you feel even harder."

Sana opened his eyes. He looked relieved, and I was grateful that I'd managed to address some of his concern.

"I mean, not to mention that you recently woke up in a world that's changed in almost every conceivable way from the one you knew." I pressed another kiss to his cheek and settled down again. We both needed to find a comfortable spot—it would be a while before my knot receded. "I can't imagine waking up tomorrow to find myself thousands of years in the future, unsure what anything was, or how I got there. I'm surprised that all of you are as adjusted as you are."

"Blaze has been a tremendous help. Without his instruction, and without Cory and Emery there to guide us, we wouldn't have been able to survive. His power allows us to blend in seamlessly almost anywhere. Cultures, customs, languages... he can absorb them all from a simple touch. It's helped us through more than one tough situation."

"Have you always spoken English?" I asked. I wanted to look down at him, but I was too exhausted and comfortable to move. I kept my head down, eyes closed. "Thousands of years ago, English wasn't a thing, was it? Did Blaze teach it to you?"

Sana snorted. He wrapped his arms loosely around me, then gave up and let them fall to the side so they rested on the floor again. "No, English wasn't a thing. I have a feeling that Blaze's power has continued to grow over time, and that he was somehow able to impart upon us the basics of this language. Or, perhaps, there's something about Emery's powers we haven't learned yet. I'm not sure."

"So not even you know the extent of your powers? You don't know how powerful you can hope to be, or what exactly you might be able to do given enough time and training?"

Sana laughed. He shook his head. "There's no end to a dragon's power except for death. If you live long enough, your gift will continue to grow with you. The oldest dragons aren't only respected because they're wise—they're respected because they are the most powerful."

"Incredible."

"Time has changed the world," Sana mused. "And it's changed all of us, too. I only hope I can learn to adapt."

"You will. And if you can't, then I'll teach you. I told you, I'll be there to protect you... and that doesn't just mean in combat."

Sana hummed. He kissed me, then sighed softly. It was a pleasant sigh, like he was letting go of everything he'd been holding inside. I found myself sighing as well, releasing pressure from my chest. The rhythm of our heartsong united us, and it washed away all the ills we'd been keeping pent up inside.

"Just promise me you'll be safe," I said after a long silence. "Promise me that you'll be one of those wise old dragons with untold power. That's all I ask of you."

Sana paused. Then he chuckled. "I'll do my best, Peter, but I can offer you nothing more than my word."

13

PETER

*I*n the early hours of the morning the day after we'd checked in, we assembled as a team in the woods behind the motel. Sammy, nervous as ever, snapped our armbands into place himself and checked to make sure each of our cloaking devices was activated. When he made it to me, I stopped him and looked him in the eyes. "It's going to be okay."

"How is this going to be okay?" he asked, unafraid to speak his mind. "We're about to sneak into the heart of enemy territory to rescue a man we don't even know, our plan is patchwork at best, and there's every reason in the world to think that we're not going to make it out of this."

"Except there's every reason in the world to think we'll make it out of this," I countered. "You're standing here with three dragon warriors, their equally as capable dragon king, and a reformed enemy who knows what's going on in that base, even if he's never been in it. You've gotten in touch with your own dragon, too."

Sammy made a face, the same one he'd made at me when we were kids and he knew I was right about something. I laughed and clapped him on the back, and he went on with making sure each of us was prepared to fly.

It was time to get going.

I looked at Sana, who was subtly keeping an eye on Cory. When he felt eyes on him, he looked my way. He didn't smile with his lips, but there was an affectionate sparkle in his eyes that made my heart skip a beat. The heartsong was the strangest thing. I'd never fallen immediately in love with a man, but I had no regrets. My heart knew what it wanted—it was up to my mind to follow suit.

"I'll be hiding us from view," Cory said once Sammy was done distributing the armbands. "We're going to land in the safest spot we can find, dress silently, then follow Sam's lead to wherever he can most easily access the compound's security systems. Peter, do you have a rough idea of where the captive omega might be located?"

"Yes," I said. "The floor plan should be fairly straightforward. I'm confident that I can get us there."

"Then once Sam's done with dismantling security, you'll be responsible for getting us into the building and to the room or cell the omega is being held captive in."

I nodded.

"Everyone will need to remain silent during this time, and we'll need to be cautious and tread lightly. This is not the time for jokes, my friends. An innocent life is depending on us."

"And what of us, Cory?" Brick asked. "What purpose will Sana, Blaze, and I serve?"

"The three of you are our backup plan," Cory said. "I will join your ranks. Should anything go wrong, we'll be the ones who keep everyone safe. We will not lose a life on this mission, neither our own nor the captive omega we've set out to rescue."

"And if we can't find the omega?" Brick asked cautiously. He cracked his knuckles, then craned his neck from side to side, likely getting ready to take flight. "What if he's been trans-ported... or has already been disposed of?"

"Then we'll send the building up in flames from the inside," Cory replied. "We'll make sure that nothing remains."

"Understood."

With nothing left to address, the dragons stripped while I

acted as pack mule. I wasn't bringing along a bag this time—I was going to clip everything to the harness that would keep me strapped down on Sana's neck. While Sana transformed and I secured my harness to him, the warriors brought me their clothes one by one so I could clip them in place. Blaze brought Sammy's, who was doing his best to hide behind the cover of the trees.

"Let's hope that Sana hasn't screwed the sense out of you," Blaze said with a wink as he delivered both his and Sammy's clothing. "We're going to need you firing on all cylinders once we land. Can you handle the heat?"

"My entire adult life has been a nonstop inferno." I clipped his clothes into place. "I'm as ready now as I'll ever be."

"Then let's take to the sky, hunter!" Blaze bumped his fist over his heart, his eyes locked with mine. I took it to be a draconian sign of respect and mimicked the symbol in return. Blaze grinned. "To flawless victory."

"To flawless victory," the men in our entourage echoed.

Then we got ready to fly.

WE DIDN'T HAVE AS FAR to travel this time as we did when we came to Colorado. The wind was still bitterly cold, and the flight was uncomfortable, but I was able to stand my own without heavy, cumbersome protective gear. With some thick gloves, a protective pair of goggles for my eyes, and some insulating, full-body underwear, I was able to withstand the temperatures just fine.

It occurred to me that, one day, I'd be taking to the skies just like Sammy was doing. Out of all the dragons, he was the most uncertain about himself—flapping a little too hard and bobbing in the sky while the others progressed smoothly—but he was also the newest to his true self.

Dragons.

All this time, I'd been told they were evil, not realizing that I was one myself.

We soared toward Sampson Peak, Cory leading the way. I'd always thought that the base would be located on top of the mountain, maybe sunken into a man-made crater or placed on a cliff in an area inaccessible to hikers. As we approached, I learned that I was wrong. There was a perilously steep cliff-face on one side of the mountain, so steep and flat that only the most skilled rock climbers would even dare attempt to scale it. It was hard to tell from so far up, but I was almost certain that the terrain offered little to no footholds. If it wasn't for the yawning cave mouth dimly lit with reflective signage toward the top of the cliff, I would have thought that no one had ever been there before.

I may have been mistaken about the compound's exact location, but I had been right about one thing—the only way we were ever going to get in or out of there was if we flew.

Cory led the way forward, guiding us toward the mouth of the cave. It was huge—more than large enough to fit five adult dragons with plenty of room to spare. Guiding a helicopter inside would require precision, but it wouldn't be an impossible task. It looked like the hunters had hollowed out the mountain for their purposes. It was better for us that way, I supposed. Once we got the omega out, the others could set fire to the base without it being seen from the neighboring city of Denver. The smoke would be contained, and when it did eventually leak out of the cave, we'd be long gone.

All of the dragons touched down. I undid my harness as quietly as I could, then unclipped each dragon warrior's clothing and handed it to them as they came to me. They dressed in total silence, and as they did, I familiarized myself with the outside of the Alpine Compound.

LED lights ran along either wall of the cave, leading helicopters inward. Similar lights ran in tracks on the ground and ceiling, likely to make it clear to helicopter pilots how much clearance they had. The atmosphere was gloomy and dark, disrupted only by the rows of LEDs that cast unnaturally white light into a place the sun had never touched. In the far

ALPHA DECEIVED | 105

distance, the cave was bathed in artificial light. I guessed that we'd find the base there.

Tactically, I knew that the location of the base was working to our disadvantage. If things got tense, breaking through the roof and darting off through the skies wasn't an option. There was only one way in, and one way out. We'd have to make sure that we watched our sixes—if they came at us from behind, they could trap us easily. We'd fight until the end to get out, of course, but I knew security here was intense, and with the destruction of the Pacific Compound—the base I had served at—I was sure that they were on high alert.

Since the Master Guardian had come into power, security was the best it had ever been. While working as a hunter, his new rule had been wonderful. Now that I was on the opposite team? And especially now that I had a pregnant dragon mate to worry about? The skillful way he ran the Hunters' Guild bothered me more than I could say.

Once everyone was dressed, Sammy and I took the lead. Sammy was nervous. The jerky, hurried way he moved betrayed him—it was the same way he'd acted when he was a kid, and even though he kept his expression impassive, I saw right through him. I wanted to tell him that it was going to be okay, but I didn't want to risk speaking. We had enough on the line as it was without giving ourselves away.

As we approached the light at the end of the cave, I saw the base more clearly. Flood lights—the kind you might find at a football field—lit the area up and cast long, eerie shadows across the natural stone floor. They illuminated a squat building with sterile white siding.

No one was standing guard outside.

Sammy hurried toward the building, sticking to the shadows as best he could, even though Cory was cloaking us. He rounded the building and came to a stop in front of a small metal box. I stood by as he lifted the lid and took a tiny dongle with a strange connector from his armband pocket. He plugged it into one of the slots in the metal box, then set his hand on the metal and closed his eyes. He tilted his head forward, and for a moment, I thought he was going to lose consciousness. Seconds before I was about to step forward to catch him, Sammy lifted his head again and looked me in the eyes. There was a look on his face that I wasn't familiar with —like he was looking through me instead of at me. He pointed toward the front door and made a thumbs-up.

It was time for me to take over.

I'd only seen the Alpine Compound's blueprints. Originally, I'd assumed that the multi-floored base was accessible through the bottommost floor and rose upward. Now I knew better. The base drilled down into the mountain like a screw twisted into wood. If we were going to burn it down, we'd need to make sure we infiltrated its lowest point, or we'd never get it all. It wasn't impossible, but it was going to be a lot harder than I'd originally anticipated.

At this point, I didn't trust any of the doors to be safe to use, but there were no windows, and it wasn't like we could crash through the ceiling. I held my hand out, fingers stretched and palm flat, to tell the others to stop and wait while I investigated. They obeyed, so I silently made my way toward the door on my own.

There were cameras set up by the door, but they didn't move to follow me. I trusted Sammy's technological know-how and I didn't let the cameras bother me—with that tiny dongle and whatever dragon magic he'd used, he'd dismantled the security systems. I knew it. My brother wouldn't let me down.

The sliding doors leading into the building had glass panels. I didn't like the idea that the doors ran on an electrical circuit, but if the power blew after we started to destroy the base, we'd simply break them down. I didn't think there were many things in the human world that could hold back an adult dragon.

I didn't see any guards on the other side of the door. I noticed a few more cameras running their programmed circuits, but otherwise, the entrance was empty. It was early in the morning—an hour or so before the early birds even thought about getting out of bed—but I found it odd that there was no one standing guard. Was that normal for a base in such an isolated location, or was something else going on? I wished that I'd been sent to the Alpine Compound before I'd burned my bridges with the Hunters' Guild, if only so that I would have known.

If it was a trap, then it was safest we face it together. Divided, our power was less than what it was combined. If the hunters were waiting in ambush around the corner, then we would face them together.

I looked over my shoulder at the group of dragons waiting for my permission to approach. I swept my hand toward the door a few times to usher them forward, then braced myself for what was about to happen. When we stepped through the doors, any number of things could go wrong. I hoped that they wouldn't, but I knew better than to invest my faith blindly. If I stayed on my toes, I could protect Sana should anything happen.

I refused to let him come to harm.

While the dragon warriors assembled, I stepped forward. Usually, my presence would trigger the sensor on the door, which would slide open, but nothing happened at all. I waved my hand, only to have Sammy grab me by the wrist and shake his head. He gestured at the small pouch strapped to my arm. The device inside of it prevented any sensors or other technological equipment from noticing our presence, I remembered.

It looked like we were going to have to use some force earlier than I would have liked.

My fingers worked their way into the tiny gap between the doors, forcing them apart. I pushed the doors apart and held them open while the rest of the team ducked beneath my arms and headed through. Brick, who was the last one through the doors, met my gaze once he was on the other side. He said nothing, but his expression was serious and thankful, and it made me feel like I had a shot at becoming a respected member of their small group.

I ducked through the doors and let them close behind me. The hallway was silent, and a chill crept down my spine. There was something wrong here, and it made the air stuffy and stagnant. Where were the guards? Where was the security? Where was *anything*?

I didn't have long to wonder what was going on. We were on a time-sensitive mission, and delaying would only make matters worse. We needed to get the omega, burn the place down, and get out—there was no time for hypotheticals. The base was what it was, and we had to adjust and keep moving.

I squared my shoulders, ignored the feeling that something was wrong, and pushed onward. There was an innocent man captured inside whose well-being depended on us, and even though I didn't know him, I wouldn't let him down.

14

SANA

We moved silently, making our way down hallways and winding staircases. Every second seemed to stretch, and I was more cognizant than ever of how loud my footsteps sounded in the total silence.

We followed the stairs down all the way, sinking deeper into the bowels of the earth with each step. When we arrived at the bottom landing, Peter held his hand out to stop us, then opened the door slowly and peeped down the hall. I waited, hair standing on end, for something to happen to him. Ever since we'd landed, my dragon had been screaming at me to protect my mate and keep him safe... but Peter was the only one who had an idea of how this base was laid out, and if he didn't lead the way, we would be lost.

It was a miserable feeling.

Peter opened the door the rest of the way, then waved us through. There was a long hallway on the other side lined with doors. Each door was equipped with a small glass window, not even wide enough that I'd be able to stick my arm through, provided I shattered the pane. I peeped into the first window to the right and found a windowless cell on the other side. There was a cot with a thin mattress, a pillow that was little better than cardboard, and a toilet beside which stood a tiny water fountain.

There was no prisoner inside.

Blaze and Sam were a little farther ahead. I watched as they checked a few more windows and moved on. It looked like the place was empty. Had we come to the wrong location, or had the Alpine Compound been evacuated before we'd arrived?

As a group, we continued down the hall. All of the rooms had the same layout, and none of them contained any prisoners. The last door was at the very end of the hall, located straight ahead of us instead of to the left or right. Peter approached it and peeped through the window, and I found myself slipping in beside him to give it a look, too.

The room was large. Its ceiling arched overhead, and although its walls were barren and white, I got the feeling that it wasn't a typical cell. What did the hunters need so much space for? And what were they planning to do with it? There were no tables, no shelves, no cabinets... but the room wasn't empty. In the center of the floor, seated on a wooden chair with his back to the door, was a young man.

Peter lifted a hand, pointed through the window, and gave us a thumbs-up. I heard the others approach from behind, preparing themselves to sweep in and grab the omega. Cory's illusion still made us invisible, and we hadn't encountered a soul along the way to the prisoner's quarters that had detected us. As far as I knew, we were safe.

It was the easiest mission I'd ever been on... and I couldn't help but feel like I was missing something. The Hunters' Guild was powerful enough to have three compounds scattered across North America, one of which had been built inside of a mountain. How was it possible that an organization like that could have such lax security? Even Cory, thousands of years divided from his rule, had three bodyguards to protect him at all times. Why was no one patrolling the halls here?

I had a sneaking suspicion that it was more than luck. Something was going on here, but I couldn't figure out what it was.

Peter lifted a hand, making sure all of us saw it. Moving deliberately, he touched the door handle. Then, cautiously, he pushed.

The door swung open.

For a moment, none of us moved. I don't think any of us had expected that it would be this easy. Had Sam's gadget de-activated the locks on the doors? I didn't know the capabilities of modern technology, so I couldn't tell for sure... but the situation made me uneasy. All of it felt far too coincidental.

When no guards burst onto the scene to investigate the opened door, and when no alarms blared, Peter lifted a hand and pointed into the room. He led the way, stepping forward quietly. Nothing happened to him when he entered the doorway, and nothing happened to him after he crossed the threshold. As a former member of the Hunters' Guild, I figured that he'd know the risks he was taking by stepping into the room. If he'd entered without a problem, the rest of us were cleared to do the same.

I stepped in next, taking the risk myself so Blaze and Brick didn't need to. Nothing happened to me, either. The hairs on the back of my neck continued to stand on end, but that didn't deter me from falling into line beside Peter as he silently moved away from the doorway and toward the omega sitting on the wooden chair.

The others entered behind us.

The omega didn't hear us, nor did he seem to sense our presence. All I could tell from where I stood was that he was young—barely an adult, if I had to guess. Eighteen, maybe nineteen. Certainly no older than his mid-twenties. His narrow shoulders were totally relaxed, and I had to wonder if he was sleeping. There was no way I'd be so composed if I were being held hostage... or maybe he was used to imprisonment. I realized I had no idea how long he'd been held captive.

One of us would need to reveal ourselves so that we could talk to him and get him out. He'd need to be filled in quickly, because once we were on the move, he'd see some serious shit. Blaze was too much of a talker to be succinct, and Brick had never exactly been the best conversationalist. I wouldn't ask our king to step forward and expose himself, and Peter and Sam were still too uneducated in our ways to know what to say. It looked like the task of enlightening the omega quickly and efficiently so we could get the hell out was on me.

I stepped forward, ready to take initiative, when something caught my eye. There was a small metal device on the omega's temple, no bigger than a penny, and every bit as round. I knew that some humans wore glasses to help them see, and I was already familiar with piercings and body modifications from my days in Novis, but I was unfamiliar with what I was seeing.

Before I could ask, Brick brushed by me. He didn't mask his footsteps, and he moved urgently. I couldn't understand why. He reached out to grab the omega by the shoulder, but before he could touch the young man, he was thrown violently across the room by an invisible force. He yelped in surprise, but the sound ended abruptly when his body crunched against the cell wall. He fell in a heap to the floor.

All of us sprang into action at once. Blaze had Cory, and that meant that it was up to me to take care of Brick. I darted across the room, running harder than I ever had before, and dropped down to Brick's side. I dipped my finger into the trickle of blood streaming from the back of his head, then pressed the coppery liquid to the tip of my tongue. My draconian gift picked up on the trauma done to him, and I quickly mapped his body, exploring every wrong done.

Broken bones, bruised organs, internal bleeding...

I watched in distress as Brick's natural defense mechanism activated—the same one that had entrapped us in stone for thousands of years. His body began to solidify from the head down, protecting his vulnerable human skin as his body slipped into stasis. I pressed my hands against his chest, trying desperately to work with his blood to reverse some of the damage done and bring him back to a conscious state, but before I could, Peter bellowed, and I felt an eerily familiar gust of wind sweep across the floor. Blaze and Cory had to be letting their dragons free... but why?

I turned my head to look over my shoulder, expecting to see Blaze's stunning blue scales, or Cory's dazzling black and red coloring. Instead, I saw something I wasn't prepared for—a dragon with snow-white scales now occupied the room.

The omega was gone.

"RUN!" Blaze shouted, but it was already too late. The dragon lifted its head, let loose an ear-splitting shriek, then rushed forward and attacked.

15

PETER

*T*he white dragon lunged in our direction, and if it hadn't been for my quick reflexes, his powerful jaw would have snapped me in half. As soon as I'd seen him rushing in my direction, I'd darted to the side and rolled out of the way, but I felt the rush of air as he passed me, ready to attack. Wickedly thin, sharp teeth curved outward, reminding me of a venomous snake. His scales reflected the harsh overhead light and glittered, almost blinding, the pure white marred only by the fearsome black claws that pierced the unfinished cement floor.

I recovered from my duck and roll and popped back onto my feet in time to see an explosion of color. A wind whipped through the room and grew so intense that I was almost knocked backward. A terrible noise, like a spaceship ripping through a wind tunnel, pierced my eardrums. The two remaining dragons—Blaze and Cory—had unleashed their dragons so rapidly that I barely saw the transition between man and beast.

Blaze, his blue scales gleaming in the overhead LEDs, screeched as he fearlessly lashed out at the white dragon. His teeth crunched into the white dragon's neck, sinking through his thick, armored scales. The white dragon screeched and thrashed his head to the side in an attempt to escape Blaze's bite, but Blaze held on. While he did, Cory tackled the dragon to the ground.

What was I supposed to do against something like that?

I looked across the room to find Sana struggling to lift Brick— now a stone statue instead of flesh and blood—from the floor. I rushed across the room to help him, hoping we could evacuate while the others fought, but the second I arrived at Sana's side, a pulse ran through the floor like cranked bass at a concert. I lifted my head in time to see a flash of blue whiz by to the left. Blaze slammed against the wall, rattling the whole room. A crack tore through the ceiling, and pieces of it started to crumble. A hunk of material the size of my head plummeted from the overhead crack and smashed into pieces a few feet from where I stood.

At this rate, we weren't going to have to burn the place down —it would collapse in on itself.

"Sana!" I cried. I grabbed Brick by the legs, taking some of the weight to help Sana carry him, but Sana shook his head. His eyes were watery.

"There's no time," he uttered. He set Brick down, gave me one last look, then abandoned his human form. There was no buffer period between being human and being dragon—his skin tore as his bones rushed to take on their new shapes, and I heard the horrific noise of his body tearing itself apart. Sana screamed in pain, but the sound was cut short when his jaw changed and could no longer accommodate the noise. His insides were changing, too, I realized—forced to move and grow before they were ready.

I saw the pain in his eyes, and it ripped me apart, too.

"Sana!"

In a flash of black scales tinted with purple, Sana was gone. He tore across the room and launched himself at the white dragon. Cory was no longer there—it looked like when Blaze had been thrown across the room, he'd been repelled, too. He'd crumpled into a pile on an opposite wall, slowly stirring as the shock of impact wore off.

Sana jumped into action to protect him.

If the Hunters' Guild had been in the possession of a dragon all this time, why hadn't I known about it? Why hadn't we *all* known about it? And why would the Master

Guardian want to keep such an allegedly dangerous creature alive?

We can't kill him, Cory's voice echoed in my head, and I tore my eyes away from the fierce battle between Sana and the white dragon to watch as Cory lifted himself from the ground. *His mind is closed off... I can't communicate with him. Something is wrong.*

No fuck something's wrong! The fucker is trying to kill us! Blaze snarled.

We need to retreat. Something has to be blocking him off from us. He's not being vicious of his own will.

I've got Brick. Cory, get the hell out of here right now.

Blaze lurched up from the pile he'd been lying in and made haste to my location, picking Brick up with his mouth. His six-inch teeth scraped against the stone, but his touch was remarkably gentle. He shot me a look. *Get the hell out of here, meatbag. You want to be that omega's lunch?*

"Where's Sammy?" I asked, my heart and my head pulled in a thousand places at once.

He left already. He's not stupid. Now come on, let's go!

"What about Sana?" I shouted. My fists trembled. I felt like I was going insane. Sana was still grappling with the white dragon in the middle of the room, all claws and teeth and snarls. "He needs help!"

Sana's a big boy, sugarplum. He can take care of himself. This is his job. *Now get moving before his efforts are in vain and the white dragon eats your ass.* Blaze was already on the move for the door. It was far too small to fit a dragon, but that didn't seem to bother him. With a swipe of his claws, he tore off pieces of the wall, widening the doorway so he could fit through. Cory followed him, ducking through the doorway.

As a soldier, I knew I should have gone. My orders were clear. But as a lover, and as a future father, I couldn't leave. How was I supposed to abandon my mate when he was fighting for his life?

The smell of copper was thick on the air. The white dragon was bleeding from multiple bite wounds, staining his white scales red —but I had a feeling that he wasn't the only one who was hurting. Sana's scales were mostly black, making it harder to see the extent of his injuries, but his scales were glossy in a way they hadn't been before—wet with blood. The white dragon attacked him merci- lessly, gnashing at Sana's shoulder as Sana struggled to pin him.

Another pulse ran through the floor, and some more debris tumbled from overhead. Before I could comprehend what was happening, Sana was repelled from the white dragon. He crashed into the wall, just like the others had. Another crack split the ceiling, and a whole section of it came down at once. It crushed one of Sana's legs, and Sana shrieked in pain.

No!

I couldn't stand by and let this happen. I couldn't watch as my pregnant mate risked his health, and the wellbeing of our unborn child, because he was too concerned about the life of his king. I had to take a stand, even if it meant risking my life.

"Hey, fuckface!" I shouted, raising my arms high above my head to attract the attention of the white dragon. He swung his head to the side and looked at me, breathing heavily. "Yeah, you, fuckface! You want something to eat? Come get me, big boy. I'm one tasty motherfucker!"

I had no idea if the white dragon could even understand English, but that didn't stop me from waving my arms above my head and making as much noise as possible. Sana's talent was tied to blood, and I knew he could heal himself if given enough time... I just needed to make sure that I distracted the white dragon for long enough.

It worked. The white dragon rushed at me, his fearsome jaw unhinging like a snake, like he thought he could eat me whole. Fat chance. Right before he arrived, I dove to the side and tucked myself so I rolled, then sprang to my feet. I hadn't spent my entire life as a military man, then a mercenary, to be eaten by some dragon scum.

"Missed me," I taunted. The dragon swung his head around, and when he did, I saw it—a tiny glint of silver metal on his temple, right by his eye. I didn't know what it was exactly, but I had a gut feeling that the Hunters' Guild was responsible for its placement, and that it was helping them pull the strings.

I sprinted across the room, leading the dragon toward the door. I heard the crash of its claws on the cement floor and the rush of wind from its wings. Something sparked overhead. What remained of the lights in the room flickered. The dragon took that as a cue, because in the next moment, I narrowly dodged a jet of flames shot in my direction. The floor ignited. Dragonfire was different than regular fire, and I knew it wasn't going to be extinguished anytime soon. If I touched it, I was in trouble. My draconian heritage didn't do me much good when my dragon was still slumbering in my soul, waiting to be woken up. Unless I transformed, I wouldn't be impervious to fire.

I turned on my heel and came face to face with the white dragon. The line of fire had trapped me in a corner. My only choices were to run through the flames and face severe burns, if not near-instant death, or to run directly at the white dragon in the hopes I could make it past him without getting hurt.

What choice did I have?

I balled my fists, sucked in a breath, and ran headfirst at the dragon in front of me. There was no light in his eyes—they were dull, like his soul was already dead. The last thing I saw before the dragon lifted one of its wickedly clawed hands and batted me across the room like it was a cat and I was its ball of yarn was the device still stuck to its temple.

I hit the wall and knew no more.

16

SANA

I recovered in time to see Peter fly across the room and hit the wall. His body fell in a heap onto the floor, folding in unnatural ways. The dragon inside my soul went berserk. A screech ripped itself from my belly and spilled from my tongue, wild and unrestrained. I climbed out from beneath the rubble and let loose with my dragonfire, but the white dragon was already on the move, and my flames spilled onto the floor, useless.

No one would harm my mate. I would *kill* him. I would tear the dragon limb from limb and devour the pieces, just to make sure he was truly dead.

Sana, Cory's voice said urgently. *You must retreat. We must not harm the omega. He's not in his right mind.*

The omega will die! I snarled. I didn't care who heard. As I spoke, I rushed forward to meet the white dragon, locking my claws with his in an attempt to tackle him to the ground. In a mess of wings and teeth, we tumbled together, fighting for dominance. *I'll kill him for what he's done!*

Get the hell out of that room right the fuck now, Sana! Blaze demanded. *Killing yourself isn't going to prove anything. We need you alive. Go!*

The room was going up in flames. Sparks cascaded from the ceiling, adding fuel to our dragonfire. I bit the white dragon's neck and crunched my jaw, puncturing his scales. He shrieked.

I wanted him to suffer. I wanted him to know all the pain he had caused me.

SANA! Cory shouted, and I knew it was time to go.

I let go of the white dragon's neck and left him on the floor, rushing to Peter's side instead. He was out cold, meaning that I'd have to carry him. With a dragon on our tails, I couldn't transform back into a human and lift him in my arms—I'd have to transport him as a dragon instead.

With all the delicacy I could muster in such a high-pressure situation, I scooped Peter up in my arm and clutched him against my underbelly. I needed all four feet to run, but I had no other option. He was unconscious and unable to help himself, so putting him in my mouth was out of the question —he'd sink down onto one of my teeth and bleed to death. I'd have to hope that I could move fast enough on three legs to keep us safe.

I hurried across the room, fumbling as I struggled to adjust to moving on three feet. Behind me, I heard the white dragon recovering from the damage I'd done him. He would be in pursuit in seconds, I realized as I rushed down the hallway leading back to the staircase. I didn't have much time to put distance between us.

A jet of fire shot past my shoulder, singeing my wing. I hissed but kept moving. The damage wasn't serious. I could still fly.

Cory and Blaze had knocked out the doorway leading to the stairway, widening it enough for me to fit through. The stairwell was narrow enough that I couldn't fly up it, but when I looked up, I saw the railings were scratched and in some places, broken. Sam, Blaze, and Cory had hopped from railing to railing so they could climb upward quickly.

I'd do the same.

I jumped just in time to miss the next jet of fire, and as soon as I had a foothold on the railing, I launched myself upward, springing to the railing behind me. With just one front hand to work with, it was a daunting task—and making sure Peter stayed safe tucked against my underbelly made it even more challenging. When the white dragon saw what I was doing and followed me, it became more harrowing yet. Columns of fire shot by me, sometimes singeing my scales, sometimes missing me. The compound's lower levels were going up in flames. Teeth gnashed at my tail, but only managed to graze it. I snatched it up toward my body and kept going. I had to make sure Peter was safe. I had to make sure that he didn't succumb to his injuries.

My heart *needed* him.

By the time we reached the top and I found the doorway Blaze and Cory had busted open, the stairwell was an inferno. The sweltering heat would soon start to melt metal and warp other heat-resistant substances. I needed to get Peter out before it got that bad.

We rushed down the hallway toward the front doors, but the white dragon was still in pursuit. He botched his landing on his last jump and thudded on the floor, giving me a precious few extra seconds to put distance between us. I scrambled forward as fast as I could. If I could just make it through the ruins of the sliding doors into the cave itself, I could spread my wings and take flight. As soon as I was airborne, I wouldn't have to worry about speed anymore—not even Peter's added weight would hold me back.

Flames ignited around my feet seconds before I burst through the open doorway. I launched myself out of them, jumping into the air and spreading my wings the second I'd cleared the building. My momentum propelled me, and I cut through the air at higher speeds than ever before. My heart pounded against my ribcage, and I was sure if Peter were awake, he would have felt it even though my armored scales.

Where are you? I asked desperately.

Blaze replied quickly. *Outside the cavern. We just took down a few combat helicopters. Goddamn, are these fuckers relentless. Get out here quick. We need to move!*

On my way.

I shot out of the mouth of the cavern to find that the sun had risen, and the day was well underway. I had no idea how long we'd spent in the Alpine Compound, but we'd lost the advantage of the early morning. As much as it was a detriment to our safety, it did help me spot Cory, Blaze, and Sam right away—their scales glittered in the sunlight. Blaze now clutched Brick to his chest, and Sam bobbed in the air, struggling to fly. I altered my course to fly for them, and as I did, I narrowly missed yet another stream of fire.

The white dragon was in pursuit, cutting through the sky as he followed me.

We need to take the white dragon out, I told them. *He won't stop. He'll follow us until we're all dead.*

We need to tire him out, Cory said. *Evasive maneuvers until we see him slowing. There's no way that he's as trained as any of us are. He'll wind down long before we will.*

It was a good plan except for one huge flaw—Sam.

Sam had made terrific progress in making peace with his draconian heritage and embracing the dragon in his soul, but he'd only just learned how to transform, and he was still struggling to master flight. While the rest of us could move quickly enough, he could only go at half that speed. We raced forward, trying to keep distance between us and the white dragon, but it was almost impossible with how slowly and awkwardly Sam moved.

Blaze, Sam said in desperation. *Blaze, help!*

You've got this, Sparky, Blaze said, but his voice was strained. *Keep your wings steady. Focus on keeping your body stiff and condensed, like a plank of wood. The less the wind has to travel over, the faster you're going to move. Imagine you're a knife cutting through the sky.*

He's coming, Blaze. He's coming for me!

Sparky, keep going. You can do this.

BLAZE!

I whipped my head around in time to see dragonfire scorch its way up Sam's back. He shrieked in pain, the sound slicing through the noise of the wind, and his wings went wonky. He dropped like a stone, and Blaze let loose with a soul-splitting, heart-wrenching roar that made me shiver. I knew all too well how he felt—when Peter had been hurt, I'd lost my goddamn mind. Blaze's standard reaction as a warrior was to attack whatever had done him wrong until it couldn't do him wrong anymore, but as Sam fell, I saw him give up the fight. He dove after Sam, depending on aerodynamics to catch up and rescue his mate. Cory followed, and I had no choice but to go after my king.

We shot toward the ground as a unit, watching as the details below revealed themselves. The green space beneath us was dotted with temporary buildings, and there were trails leading this way and that. As we grew closer, I saw the throngs of people—hundreds of them.

Blaze tucked himself around Sam, keeping him safe as safe as he kept Brick, then hit the ground hard. His wings had slowed his descent so the impact wasn't fatal, but it stirred up an obscuring cloud of dust that Cory and I used to mask our landing—not that it mattered much. Every person in the park we'd landed in had to have seen us dropping from the sky.

And they *definitely* saw the white dragon in hot pursuit.

The situation had gone from bad to worse, and I wasn't sure how to turn things around. If the white dragon didn't snap out of his stupor, innocent people were going to die. I had to make a choice—defy my king's word and end the life of the captive omega we'd gone to rescue, or endanger hundreds of innocent lives.

When, to my surprise, the people nearby didn't run, but cheered and drew closer, I knew what I had to do. We'd made a mistake, and now we had to fix it.

I would fight to the death. It was the only way.

17

PETER

I woke to the sound of an audience cheering, and I thought for a blissfully ignorant moment that maybe I'd been brought to a hospital, and there was some live studio audience on the television across the room. As I continued to come to and realized that there was a small, sharp stone digging into my arm, I knew that I was mistaken.

I opened my eyes and looked up at a blue sky. There were no clouds, no birds, and no planes. I turned my head to the side and found myself surrounded by people I didn't recognize, and who seemed to want nothing to do with me. Some of them were dressed in medieval period piece clothing, others in shirts and jeans.

What the hell was going on?

I sat up and blinked to clear the spots out of my eyes. My head felt like it had been split open, and my body ached. The last thing I remembered, I'd been in the captive omega's cell in the basement of the Alpine Compound, and the white dragon...

I gasped and scrambled to my feet. Where was Sana? Where were any of them?

A flash of blue directed my focus. I found Blaze, Sana, and Cory circling the white dragon. They were maybe fifteen feet away—far too close for comfort. I knew that their dragonfire could blast out that far. What the hell were civilians doing, clustering so close to a group of obviously dangerous creatures?

The white dragon lifted his head and let loose with a puff of flame. The audience went wild cheering and clapping. A young woman who stood next to me, skinny as a stick with her hair tied back in a ponytail, laid a hand on my arm. I jumped.

"I can't believe this!" she said to me enthusiastically as she adjusted her round glasses. There was a goofy smile on her face, like she'd just seen something incredible instead of the potentially lethal deathmatch going on in front of her. "This is the best show I've *ever* seen. Are you the one in charge, or are you just one of the actors?"

"What are you talking about?" I asked in disbelief.

"Oh, oh, I get it." She winked at me. "You're one of the actors, and you're not supposed to break character. I get it. That's okay—I just wanted to say that this is incredible, and I'm definitely going to be back next year! I had no idea that my general admission ticket would let me see something as amazing as this!"

"Where are we?" I demanded. I glanced back to the dragons, eager to put an end to this insanity. There were too many lives at risk.

"Um, the Unicorn Festival at Clement Park?" She frowned. Her hand dropped away from my arm. "We weren't expecting dragons, but there are some dragon-themed shops here, so I should have known something like this would happen. The organizers are geniuses. I wish I knew how you did it. Is it some kind of special CGI? Like when they projected a Tupac hologram at Coachella?"

I raked a hand down my face in total disbelief. The pieces were slotting into place. We'd somehow managed to escape the cell, and we'd likely started to retreat, only to be grounded here... at the Unicorn Festival. Now the people at the festival thought we were an attraction.

They didn't know to run because they thought our struggle was part of the show.

"You need to get back," I told her. "It isn't safe."

"Oh! I love this!" she giggled and danced back a few steps. That wasn't really what I had in mind. All of these people were seconds away from losing their lives.

"You need to get back," I said again, louder this time. I lifted my arms over my head. "Everyone, get back!"

No one was listening to me, and the dragon warriors weren't making any progress. I understood their dilemma—if they attacked, they risked enraging the white dragon, and that meant he might spew fire that would harm the people clustered around the fight or fly off the rails and attack someone. But if all they did was circle him and keep him pinned in place, the danger would never end. Someone was going to get hurt eventually.

That person might as well be me.

The white dragon had his back to me, his tail whipping back and forth like an irritated cat. I let go of my fear and ran at him. Whatever was going on had something to do with the metal device attached to his temple, and I was going to put an end to it. I sprinted through the ring of warrior dragons as the audience went wild and launched myself at the white dragon's neck. The white dragon screeched and threw his head back, lifting his long neck to try to knock me off, but I was made of tougher stuff than that. I shimmied up his neck with my arms and thighs like he was a fucking rope in a high school gym. Before I could make it to his head, an overwhelming feeling of dread pierced my heart, and I heard a cry of anguish and fear not all that far behind me.

It was Sana.

No, Sana's voice echoed in my head. *No! What are you doing? Peter, stop! You'll be injured.*

"Tough shit," I uttered, not sure if he could hear me or not. As the white dragon thrashed his head and neck from side to side, trying to shake me loose, I held tight and waited for him to calm down. The first chance I got, I shimmied up the scant distance I had left to his head and stretched my arm forward, trying to reach the circular device by his temple.

PETER!

The audience was screaming in appreciation of the show, worked into a frenzy by what they saw. Their excitement was a dull roar in my ears. I reached for the device, straining...

The white dragon spread his wings and started to flap. The gust, I realized, was meant to knock me off. I squeezed tighter with my thighs, desperately seeking traction as we started to lift off from the ground. If I could just reach a little farther...

My fingertips brushed the device. I gritted my teeth and lunged forward, losing my grip on the white dragon's body.

My fingers curled over the device, and as I fell to the ground, I ripped it from his temple. It hadn't just been stuck there—when I ripped it free, blood started to flow. On the flat end of the circular device once pressed against the white dragon's head was a metal spike that had pierced through his skull. It glistened red in the morning light.

I hit the ground hard, and in the following second, Sana was next to me. He covered me with his wings as if to shield me from the world and curled around me protectively. A rattling noise warbled in his throat, almost like a sob. It broke my heart, and I pushed my pain aside to crawl next to him and run my hands down his scales. I had no idea if it would soothe him, but I had to do something.

"I'm okay," I promised. "You need to make sure you stay safe. I don't know if what I did was enough to defeat him... you need to be alert. Be strong for us."

Sana lifted his head, and as he did, sunlight flooded into the small enclosure he'd made with his body. I was able to peek at what was happening just a few feet away.

The white dragon was gone. Instead, a small, naked young man lay wilted on the ground. It had worked. I'd removed the device, and the white dragon had fallen. Whatever technology the Hunters' Guild had used to control him was separated from him now and would no longer influence his actions.

We were safe.

There was a rush of wind as the warrior dragons shifted back to their human forms. The audience was going wild again, and I was frankly surprised we hadn't been trampled. Sana shifted back last, and when he'd regained his human form, he swept me into his arms and held me close. "Never do that again."

"Only if you promise not to, too."

He pulled back from his embrace and glared at me. I chuckled.

"Sparky," I heard Blaze utter. I looked up from Sana to find Blaze crouched beside my brother. Both of them were naked, but Sammy was curled up on himself, clearly injured. I saw burn marks down his sides and over his shoulders—he'd been hurt. "Oh fuck, Sparky... it's going to be okay. It's all going to be okay. Just be strong for a little longer. I swear, it won't be like this for long. I'm going to make sure you get better."

Sana parted from my side, taking the clearing at a run. People were wolf-whistling now, and some of them had started to mutter reproachfully about our little "performance." It looked like vicious dragons were A-OK, but nudity? Shameful. A total disgrace.

I climbed to my feet, my body already aching. Once I cooled down, I was going to be in for a world of pain. I pushed that thought aside and went to stand by Sana, who had his hands on Sammy. Sammy was whimpering, clearly hurting, and Blaze was beside himself with fear. I squeezed Blaze's shoulder, and he looked up at me with an expression more vulnerable than I'd ever seen on him before. The loudmouth joker loved my brother—I saw it plainly in his eyes.

"It will be just fine," Sana told Sammy in a comforting voice. As he spoke, I saw Sammy's injuries slowly reversing. The damage done began to fade away. I'd never seen Sana's gift at work on someone else before, and as I watched him do what he did best, I realized how amazing he really was. "It will only hurt for a little while longer. You're stronger than this. You will see it through."

Slowly, Sammy's whimpering tapered off. His injuries disappeared. Sana lifted his hands from his body and nodded at Blaze, who helped Sammy to his feet. Blaze tucked him under his arm and held him close.

"What about Brick?" Sana asked. A short distance away, I saw Brick lying still, made of solid stone.

"You and I will carry him," Cory said. He looked to me. "Peter, you'll need to carry the omega. Are you capable?"

"Yeah." I nodded. I was sore, but that wasn't going to deter me. "What are all of you going to do about clothes?"

Before anyone could answer, a large woman bustled her way

through the crowd and elbowed someone out of the way. She wore a bright pink shirt that stretched across her ample bosom, a white unicorn in mid-rear printed upon it.

"Don't worry, boys," she announced loudly. "I would never forget the cutest damned couple I've ever seen. All of you, come with me. You can't be too careful, especially at events like this. You never know when the government is looking... and at your current state of undress, you're making them blush something fierce. Let's go get you some clothes." She winked. "Us Cornies take care of each other, you know."

18

SANA

I didn't recognize the rotund woman who'd elbowed her way out of the crowd, but she seemed eager enough to help despite the fact that we were naked, bloody, and in poor shape following an intense battle. More than that, Sam, who was paranoid about everything and everyone, seemed to trust her. His eyes lit up when he realized who it was who'd stepped forward, and even though he was nude, he seemed nowhere as embarrassed as he had been before. I hadn't realized that Sam had friends, but in retrospect, I realized that notion was ridiculous—despite how particular and introverted he was, of course there had to be other people in his life outside of our small group. The woman in the pink shirt was just an unlikely candidate.

"So," the woman said as we walked. The crowd gave us a

wide berth, some gaping in amazement, others scrunching their noses in disgust. "That was one hell of a show you boys put on. To be honest, when I saw it, I wasn't sure that it wasn't a distraction. When us Cornies get together, sometimes things get... intense. It wouldn't be the first time the government's tried to intervene with one of our gatherings, and one of us had to cause a scene so they looked the other way."

"I can imagine," Blaze said conversationally. "The government's always sticking its nose where it doesn't belong."

"You're telling me!" she belly-laughed. "But when I saw Samuel over there, I knew that it was just some kind of... performance art. You have to tell me, though, who were you looking to entertain: the audience in general, or some government operatives? A show like that isn't cheap to put on. You must have had some frickin' good reasons to spend that kind of cash."

"Oh, you know... a little bit of column A, a little bit of column B." Blaze shrugged a single shoulder. He had Sam tucked beneath the other, and he wasn't letting him go. "There's a good reason for everything that happens in this world, isn't there?"

The woman in the pink shirt scoffed. "You can say that again."

"I hate to interrupt what seems to be a happy reunion... but would anyone mind explaining what's going on?" Cory asked. He had Brick's shoulders tucked under his arm. I carried him by his feet. The protective stone casing Brick's body was heavy and difficult to carry, but at least he was stiff as a board. None of us had to worry about struggling with a limp wall of muscle.

"In a second. First, we need to get out of the public area. While I appreciate the full-frontal nudity going on, I'm guessing it'll only be a matter of time until the festival organizers catch wind of all those delicious dongs you've got on display and swoop in to put an end to it. We'll want to get you men clothed before that happens."

"Delicious dongs?" I asked Cory in a low voice.

"I don't know," Cory whispered back, equally as mystified.

Peter, meanwhile, busted out in laughter. I looked his way, trying to catch onto what was being said, but all he did was shake his head. "I'm glad we found you. I didn't know that Sammy had friends in Colorado."

"He doesn't," the woman said. "At least, not that I know of. I traveled here to attend the Unicorn Festival. It only happens once a year, but it never disappoints. If I'd known to expect you, I would have told the other Cornies to save some of our pamphlets. I haven't seen Samuel on the forums or the website."

I had a vague awareness of what she was speaking about, but I kept my silence, letting my attention settle on Peter. He'd done battle with a dragon as a human—a feat as stupid as it was impressive. Perhaps I'd underestimated him. I bit the inside of my lip and let my eyes trace the muscular curves of his body. There were abrasions on his skin and I guessed that he had deep bruising—both of which I could take care of as soon as we had a moment to ourselves. With Brick, Sam, and the captive omega in such poor health, my skills were needed elsewhere first. Peter was strong, and I knew he'd survive. My heartsong never would have given me a weak mate. It knew that I needed a man just as strong and capable as I was... and it had given me Peter. Now I understood why.

"It's been a busy year," Sam admitted. He hadn't spoken much since I'd brought him back to health. He was likely exhausted and in shock—it was only natural after an event so traumatic. "Sorry."

"Nothing to be sorry about." She waved a hand dismissively, then pulled back the fabric door flap of a tall event tent and held it open for us. "Like I said, if you aren't ready to be under government scrutiny, then it's probably best that you stay off Corny sites. We're onto something, you know. Since we met last year, one of our very own Corny researchers,

Mick, has discovered a fossilized unicorn horn. We're still trying to get it looked at in a university lab. For some reason, no one's been taking us seriously."

"Perhaps because they already know the horn would reek just as badly as the unicorn it belonged to," Cory mumbled under his breath.

I wasn't in any kind of emotional state to laugh, but his comment made me smile.

"You can't trust universities," Sam said in a strained voice. "All of them are funded by the government, even if they claim they're private. The Man keeps tabs on every research project. You're best going with an independent lab... but you need to be careful about those, too."

"Mmm, good point." When we were all inside the tent, the woman closed the flap. The inside of the tent was surprisingly packed; there were a few racks of clothing—mostly brightly colored t-shirts—and a few stuffed hiking packs. Inflatable mattresses occupied one corner of the tent, blankets and pillows piled loosely on top. "Well, we're here. This is our Corny meet-up tent. All us Cornies pitched in to make it happen, and it allows those of us who can't afford a motel room to crash somewhere free for the night. The organizers weren't one hundred percent happy with us when we requested it, but they gave in eventually. This," she pointed at the racks of clothing, "is Corny merch that we're selling to spread the word. But after a show like that, I'm willing to part with some of it for free. What are your sizes?"

Sam ducked out from beneath Blaze's arm and walked sluggishly until he stood at the woman's side. "I'll... I'll take care of that. Can everyone else go rest?"

"Of course. You do look pretty tired after that performance. I'm really impressed by the quality of your fake blood, by the way. You're going to have to give me your recipe sometime... you know, for Halloween." She laughed. "The rest of you can go settle down. Your arms must be getting tired, carrying that prop and that young actor, there."

I was so distracted after what had happened that Brick's weight didn't even register. I glanced down at him, then back at the strange woman. I was nervous about Sam—he seemed exhausted to the point of collapsing—but there was nothing more I could do for him. I'd repaired his body as much as it could be repaired. The rest would be worked off with sleep and time.

"I don't need to sit," Blaze said, stepping forward to stand next to Sam. "I'm going to stay with... Samuel... here while he finds us clothes."

Sam smacked a hand to his face and held back a scathing remark. My anxiety eased. If he had enough energy to express how annoyed he was by Blaze's antics, we weren't going to have a problem.

The rest of us, however, needed some time to recover. I still needed to treat Brick and the omega, and then after that, Peter. Cory, as far as I could tell, was unscathed from our battle. For that, I was grateful. I may have failed as a dragon warrior by allowing an alpha to take my heat, but at least I'd managed to protect my king in combat.

We walked to an out-of-the-way corner of the tent and settled on the tent floor. The material was thick and had the consistency of plastic, and when I slid anything against it—my foot, my thigh, or my ass—it made a strange slick noise. It wasn't exactly comfortable, but it was certainly better than nothing.

While Sam, Blaze, and the woman set to work finding us clothing, I scooted across the floor to sit by Peter and the unconscious omega. The omega's skin was pale, and his facial features were delicate. I traced my finger through the trickle of blood still leaking from the hole in his temple and set it to my tongue. His pains became my pains, and I felt every one of his ills.

My stomach churned, and for a moment, I had to pull back. It wasn't often that I came across an injury I couldn't fix, but his wounds ran deeper than the physical. His imprisonment had left a black mark on his soul, and it was a heavy burden to carry even for someone as strong of will as I was. Whatever the Master Guardian had done to this boy, it was bad. I hoped that he would find some solace now that he was free.

I hoped that we all would.

I placed my hands on his body, pushing aside my discomfort. No one else could do this job, and I would not allow my feelings to prevent me from doing my duty. Following the map of his body, I worked with his blood to knit his wounds and repair the damage that had been done. When I was finished, I took my hands away and drew in a breath like I'd just broken the surface of the water after a prolonged dive. I was exhausted, but I still had work to do.

Brick needed me.

I slid across the floor to sit at Brick's side. My shoulders rose and fell from the exertion of practicing my gift, but I couldn't stop. I already knew the map of Brick's body, just as I knew everyone's in our small group. I accessed my memories and laid my hands on the stone that covered him, then started to repair the damage done. It was my hope that I could repair him enough that he'd wake from stasis and remove the stone armor keeping his human form safe, but the more energy I poured into healing his injuries, the more I knew it wasn't going to be so easy. Brick's spine had broken upon impact with the wall, and even as I fitted the bones back together and fused the brittle fissures, it was going to take some time before his stasis wore off. The shock alone needed to be worked off—it would likely be several days, if not several weeks, that he was dead to the world.

By the time I was finished healing Brick, sweat had beaded on my brow, and my hands were shaking. I closed my eyes and let my shoulders slump. What I needed was rest. After using my gift in such an intense way, I felt nauseous and dizzy. If I continued, I was going to be sick... or worse. But Peter needed me.

I turned to look at Peter, pushing past my own discomfort in an attempt to look strong. Peter wasn't buying it. He shook his head. "I know that you're not feeling well right now. You're not going to make yourself feel worse by trying to heal me. I've suffered worse injuries. I'll be fine."

The heartsong we shared allowed Peter to feel what I was feeling—of course he knew that I was exhausted and ill. I frowned, gazing at my bare knees. I couldn't stop shaking. "It will only take a second. You'll feel better."

"And you'll feel worse. That's not something I'm willing to agree to." Peter looked at Cory—he was the only one who could hear our conversation. "I think you know more about our situation than you're letting on. Is that right?"

"Perhaps," Cory said with a knowing smile.

"Then you'll understand why I have to ask you to get your

man to stand down. I won't accept treatment if it means that it comes as a detriment to Sana's health."

"Sana," Cory warned me. "You'll rest."

I pinched my shoulder blades together, frustrated with myself. "I'll be fine. His injuries aren't as severe as Brick and the omega's. It won't take much more."

"Sana."

I let my shoulders slump and shook my head. "Understood."

"Thank you. We're going to need you in good condition for the flight home," Cory said.

"What?" My blood ran cold. "The flight home? We haven't torched the Alpine Compound yet. The lower levels have likely been destroyed, but we did little to make sure the base's upper levels were ruined. We can't leave yet."

"Someone will need to bring Brick back to the estate," Cory said.

"Then send Blaze and Sam!" I insisted. "Sam has been injured, and he'll be more skittish than ever. Now that the infiltration has taken place, he has no need to be here."

"You are the one whose body is closest to giving out," Cory observed. "You will go home and recuperate with Brick and the omega."

I looked desperately at Peter, then back to Cory. Cory knew my secret, and he had to understand... he had to.

"I won't leave without Peter," I said. "I refuse. I can't carry the omega, Brick, and Peter all at once. Not safely. And besides, without you cloaking us, we'll be seen. It's a long way back to our estate."

"Then what do you suggest?" Cory asked. "I'm of the opinion that Sam won't want to fly again after what happened—not until Blaze builds his confidence back up. Just as you can't carry three people at once, Blaze won't be able to, either."

"Then go with him," I said. "You and Blaze will carry the others back to the estate. I'll stay here and wait for your return in the motel. It will give me some time to recover."

"Me as well," Peter said, chiming in to back me up. He slid in beside me, putting a hand on my bare back. "You, Blaze, and Sammy can go home and recover for a day or so—spend some time with your children while you rest. Sana and I will do the same here. Then we'll band together and torch the fuckers out of their hidey-hole. We'll end this."

Cory looked between the two of us, his lips thinned and his eyes worried. "I suppose it's the only choice we have. We'll return home to the estate as soon as Blaze and I are rested for the journey. Then, upon our return, we'll finish things."

It wasn't the only choice, but I wasn't about to tell him what I had planned. I knew he'd never approve of it. Instead, I nodded and let myself lean against Peter, seeking his strength and comfort.

I was going to put an end to the madness and keep my king safe, as was my duty. I only hoped that I had the strength left in me to see it through.

19

PETER

"So," the woman who stood beside Sammy said. "Who wants purple?"

Shirt by shirt, clothes were distributed. We dressed the tiny omega in clothes a little too large for him, hoping he'd stay warm. He looked frail and delicate, and he'd yet to wake up. I had to wonder if he'd gone into stasis, like Brick. The metal spike I'd pulled out of his head had to have been wreaking havoc on his body.

In the end, the dragon warriors were dressed in Corny t-shirts and printed sweatpants. There were no shoes, socks, or underwear to distribute, but it was better than nothing. At least none of us would be arrested for public indecency.

"It occurred to me that I never asked for your name," I said when the woman was done distributing Corny merchandise to the group. "I'm Peter, Samuel's brother. It's nice to meet you."

"Oh, a *brother!* And how handsome." She fanned her face with her hand, then laughed and held it toward me. I shook it. "The name's Saint Anley. I met your brother last year when he stopped by the motel I work at. His lover, there, was wearing a unicorn shirt, and I knew right away that we'd get along great. Do the rest of you happen to be Cornies, too?"

"Cornies?"

She tutted. "People who believe that unicorns once existed... and maybe do still exist. We've got a website and everything. Samuel, do you still have the info I gave you?"

"Yes," Sammy said. "All of us are Cornies at heart, even though we haven't visited that website yet."

"Maybe it's for the best, if you're putting on shows like you just did." She crossed her arms, propping up her breasts. "Well, it's all good. I know that you boys would have my back if I was ever in need."

"Of course," I said.

"Then that's all I need to know." She patted Sammy several

times on the back, then cleared her throat. "Are you sticking around? I could take you around the festival. There's a mermaid tank, and a unicorn pasture. Of course, they're not real mermaids or unicorns, but the spirit is there."

"No, no, we've got to get going," Sammy said, doing his best to sound kind. "All of us need to get cleaned up after our... *performance.* It was nice meeting up with you again."

"You too!" Saint Anley laughed. "Small world, isn't it? Who knows—maybe we'll meet up again someday."

"Maybe," I said, glancing in Sana's direction. He was run ragged after investing so much energy between fighting for his life and healing the rest of us. I saw it as plainly on his face as I did through our heartsong. "I just hope next time we'll be in a place where we can chat. It's not often I meet one of Samuel's friends."

She beamed. "We'll make plans for next year. You can send me a message through the website and we'll set something up. It'll be great!"

If going to a unicorn festival meant that I didn't have to engage in hand-to-hand combat with a heavily armored, fire-breathing creature? Yeah. That sounded pretty fucking great to me, too.

It was mid-afternoon by the time we made it back to our motel room. Each of us split up, retreating directly to our rooms for much-needed rest. Cory had taken custody of Brick, who was still in stasis, and Blaze and Sammy had elected to take care of the unconscious omega. Sana slid the key card into the lock on the door, then twisted the handle and let us inside. I held out a hand in parting to Blaze and Sammy, who were struggling with their key card on the door next to ours. Blaze held the omega in his arms, ever gentle with him. I knew that the omega and my brother were in good hands with Blaze, and I didn't doubt for a second that they'd be taken care of while they recovered.

Even though we'd walked into a disaster and almost lost our lives, everything was going to be okay.

As soon as the door closed behind us, Sana let out an exhausted sigh and trudged toward the bathroom. I followed, not wanting to leave him be when he was so weak. "Sana, stop. Let me help you."

He looked up at me, the fight gone from his eyes. "Sure."

"What happened isn't your fault, you know. None of us could have guessed that the Hunters' Guild would use a fucking dragon against us. For as long as I worked for them, we were told that dragons were something we had to destroy. I don't know what happened to change that."

"I knew that something was wrong, but I didn't say anything," Sana said. He continued on his way to the bathroom, and I followed him through the door. "If I'd spoken up, maybe no one would have been hurt. We could have approached the omega more cautiously."

"We already approached him pretty fucking cautiously," I said. "No matter how careful we were, or how many traps we were expecting, I don't think we would have known to expect a dragon. It was a shitty situation, but we dealt with it, and all of us made it out alive, even if some of us were injured."

A shiver ran down Sana's spine. "One wrong move and we might not have. We could have ended the danger if we'd killed the white dragon, but none of us wanted to take his life —we knew there was something wrong with him. We let ourselves be hurt to protect him. Someone could have died..."

"Sana..." I squeezed his shoulder and turned him so that he was looking at me. I gazed into his eyes, but he refused to look at me. "You can't beat yourself up over something that could have happened. The fact is, it didn't. That's all that matters. We need to move on with our lives and learn from that experience. Next time, we'll know better. That's all we can ask for."

Sana blinked away tears. "You could have died. You aren't even able to transform yet, and I led you straight into a hostile dragon's den. He could have ripped you to pieces, or charred you alive. He could have crushed your bones with his teeth, or shredded you like wet paper..."

"Sana," I said, more firmly than before. I felt his sorrow welling inside, and it leached into me and made me uncertain of what we'd just done. I'd allowed my pregnant mate to go into combat. I'd let him exhaust himself healing others when he needed all the energy he could get as his body changed to accommodate our child. What if he'd been seriously injured? What if he'd died? "You don't have to worry about me. You never have to worry about me. All I want is for you to be safe."

I pulled him to me, and he buried his head against my chest. Both of us were sweaty and bruised from the fight with the white dragon, but I didn't care. Right now, all I needed was to feel Sana's heartbeat and breathe in his scent. I needed to know that he was still here, and that I still had him.

Now more than ever, I needed to keep him safe. I needed to end this insanity with the Hunters' Guild before it endangered my mate again.

"I was so fucking scared of losing you," Sana whispered. His fingers tightened, snagging my shirt. "My dragon was going out of his mind. I... I thought that the white dragon would kill you. I saw you die a million different times in my mind's eye. I can't let this go on."

"I can't let it go on, either," I told him in a whisper. I kissed the side of his head, remembering the metal spike the Master Guardian had driven through the omega's temple. If they caught Sana, would he suffer the same fate? Would he become a mindless slave to an organization with unclear goals? "We're going to end this."

"I'm going to return to the compound once they're gone," Sana whispered. He didn't let me go. "I'm going to burn it to the ground. No one is going to be put at risk again. I won't have you, or anyone else, put in harm's way again."

"We're going together," I said. "I'm not letting you do this on your own."

"You can't transform. What could you do? No man would stand a chance."

"Then teach me how to transform, and we'll burn it down together." I pulled back to look him in the eyes so he'd know I was serious. "I'm ready. I want to help you, and I need to keep you safe. I can do this."

Sana frowned and shook his head. "You saw Sam... he's had practice with his wings, and he's still not very capable as a dragon just yet. You'll need more time and practice."

I shook my head. "I love Sammy, and I think he's a fantastic, practical individual who is... highly motivated if the situation

ALPHA DECEIVED | 161

is right… but he's not a trained warrior. He doesn't have the discipline I do. It wouldn't be the first time that I've been asked to perform in a high-pressure situation with minimal training. And if this is something that's already in my soul—if it's something I was born to do—then I know I can do this. I can help you burn that base to the ground. I can help keep you safe."

Sana, who always looked so independent and in control of himself, broke. Tears streamed down his cheeks, their paths wiping clear the grime on Sana's face. He brushed his tears away with the back of his hand.

"You're not in this alone anymore, Sana," I told him. "You don't have to be the only one harboring your secret. I'm here, and I'm going to make sure that you get the job done so you can move on to the next stage of your life satisfied with the service you've given Cory."

"You're injured, though," Sana said. "You must be tired, too. We just went through hell trying to keep that dragon contained."

I winked. "Military training."

Sana shook his head and sighed, and I laughed.

"Come on, heartsong," I said, calling him what I'd heard Cory call his mate. It felt right, and when Sana smiled for me, it felt even better yet. "Let's hop in the shower, get you into some clothes that don't have unicorns on them, then get to work. We've still got a couple hours left before the sun sets, and I know just how to use them."

20

SANA

*P*eter stood, nude, in a clearing in the woods behind the motel. The intricate designs of his tattoos still captured my eye, and I focused on them while he rolled his shoulders out and loosened his body for what we were about to do. We'd wandered far enough away from the building and the road that I didn't think it likely that anyone would happen by.

"You've got to let go," I told him. "Inside of you, you'll see flashes of the dragon... usually the color of your scales, or a flickering of flame. You need to do your best to ignore it and pretend that it isn't there."

"That sounds counterproductive. Isn't the point to get my dragon to come out? If I ignore it, it's never going to emerge."

"That's the thing." I smiled at him, enjoying the way the setting sun shaded his muscles. "You want the dragon to feel like a natural extension of your body. You don't walk around all day noticing the point of your nose, do you? Or thinking about how much your arm weighs, and how strange it is that they swing when you walk?"

Peter scrunched up his face in concentration, eyes closed. "No."

"It's the same thing with the dragon. If you want it to be a natural part of you, you have to make it feel like it belongs... and that means you need to ignore it. Pretend it's nothing new. You don't see it in your field of vision any more than you do your nose."

"I think I've got it." Peter let out a slow, steady breath. "So all I need to do is not focus on it and it'll come out? That's the secret?"

"It's a little more than that," I admitted. "It's a delicate balance between recognizing its presence inside of you and integrating it into your soul. Your dragon has been dormant all these years, so he might be a little slow to wake up, especially considering your age."

"I'm thirty-one," Peter argued. "I'm not that old."

"Most dragons are awoken in their teenage years," I said

gently. "Yours will be sluggish. It might take a bit more effort than it would a younger man."

"Screw that." He furrowed his brow harder than before and clenched his fists. I couldn't help but smile. His determination was endearing. "I can do this. Some teenage punk isn't going to best me."

"Some teenage punk also knew about his draconian heritage his whole life, and was brought up around other adult dragons. You're at a double disadvantage here."

"Not helping, Sana."

I choked back a chuckle. "Sorry. You know I believe in you. That's your power, isn't it? That you can detect the truth?"

"Yup," Peter said between clenched teeth. "And I can also detect when you're trying to be a pest."

I pressed a hand over my mouth, not confident that I'd be able to hold back my laughter.

"Is there anything else I have to know?" he asked. "When I'm transforming, is there something I need to do? Something I should avoid doing? Any advice for a first-time dragon you think it wise to impart before we get this party started?"

"No." I paused. "Well, except don't try to transform in a space that won't fit your dragon. More houses have been destroyed that way than I can count. It was a problem for a while in Novis—young, dumb teenagers challenging each other to transform in as small a space as possible. Houses were knocked to the ground as support walls gave out, property damage was done, and some young dragons even lost their lives when they tried to transform in tight caves only to crush themselves to death when the rock wouldn't shatter to accommodate them."

"Good to know that dumb teenagers aren't just a now thing," he said, voice just as strained as it'd been before. "And I thought eating laundry detergent pods was stupid."

"I don't know what you're talking about."

"It's fine. Half the time, I don't think I know, either."

I saw his arms tense. His shoulders tightened. A shudder ran down his spine. He was trying hard to transform, but by putting such pressure on himself, he was only making the process more difficult.

"You need to relax," I told him. "Straining won't wake your dragon. Open yourself up from the inside. Delve into the deepest parts of yourself that you usually don't allow yourself to access. You'll find him there."

I wished there was something else I could do, but the process was truly an individual journey. Back when Novis had been in its full glory, there'd been certain plants we'd used to help access that deep part of our souls—mind-altering substances to help bridge the connection between the body and the spirit. Without those plants, Peter was on his own.

"I see something," Peter said. "It's... scaly? It keeps moving in my peripheral vision."

"Perfect!" I beamed. "You're on the right track. You've found your dragon. Now, keep that part of yourself in mind, but don't focus on it. Allow it to become a part of you. Let it blend with who you are."

"For how long?"

"For however long you want to remain in your dragon form," I told him. "Once you've familiarized yourself with how transformation feels, you can work on the speed at which you transform... but right now, you're looking at a slow transformation. Take it one step at a time. Allow it to wash through you, and keep urging it forward even after your wings appear."

I admired him for his dedication and appreciated the sentiment behind what he was doing. Peter was putting in energy he didn't have to make sure I didn't have to fight alone. As long as I lived, and for as long as we were together, I didn't think I'd ever be able to properly express how much that meant to me.

"Shit," Peter grunted. "Okay... okay. I'm starting to go numb. Is this a normal feeling, or am I killing myself somehow?"

"Numbness is good. Your body numbs itself before it goes through a transformation so that you don't have to endure the pain. That's good. You're almost there. Keep it up."

"It's really fucking weird," Peter grumbled. "I've got pins and needles all over."

"Where? I'll take them out for you."

"Right. Ancient dragon from thousands of years ago... I keep forgetting. Pins and needles is just a saying."

"Well, whatever it is, you're doing a fantastic job. Keep going!"

I saw Peter's shoulders push out to the side, the first sign that transformation was about to occur. Then, slowly, I witnessed his wings emerge from his back. Blood-red scales, heavily armored and beautifully shaped, lined the fingers of his wings, and the membrane stretching between each was a translucent black that made my heart skip a beat. I'd always found red scales to be attractive, and while I was proud of my noble black and amethyst coloring—a royal coloration exclusive to Novis—I'd secretly harbored jealousy for Cory, whose scales were tipped with red instead of purple. To see scales that color on my mate stirred my cock to life, and I shifted my thighs to try to hide my excitement.

When Peter's wings emerged in full, his beautiful blood-red scales continued to spread. They plunged down his back and over his shoulders. As they did, his bones and muscles began to stretch and change, readying themselves to fit his new body. I watched in awe as my mate tackled transformation for the first time with flawless ease.

Peter's body curled in on itself—a natural step in the process. A tail grew, strong and sturdy. Black claws emerged, piercing the ground he stood on. At last, he opened his mouth and stretched his new jaw, revealing a row of wickedly pointed teeth. The flecks of red-amber in his eyes had intensified, and I found him beyond gorgeous.

How do I talk? Peter asked. His mouth bobbed awkwardly, but no sound came out. I snickered. *What the fuck? I'm not making any noise at all. How do I use my vocal cords? How the hell am I going to tell Sana if I can't figure out how to change back?*

"I can hear you," I said, not wanting to cause him any more undue psychological dread. No matter how funny his internal monologue was, he deserved to know that he wasn't all on his own. "All you need to do is imagine that you're talking. You don't have to open your mouth—in fact, until you learn how to control your fire, it's probably better that you keep your mouth closed as often as you can. Whenever you think words like you'd speak them, surrounding dragons will be able to hear you."

How far is the reach? Peter asked.

Far enough that you're fucking reaching our bedroom, Blaze shot back. *Sana, for the love of the kingdom, teach him about filters. Some of us are trying to soothe our very frightened, very injured mates.*

I'm not that injured, Blaze. Sana healed me.

You were hurt, and I'm going to dote on you until I know for certain that you're not hurting anymore, Sparky. You'll just have to live with it.

Peter dipped his head—a sign of embarrassment—and looked at me for guidance. It looked like he was going to hold his silence until I taught him to filter his thoughts.

I smiled, doing my best to put positive energy into the channel between our souls. "After transforming as easily as you did, setting up a filter won't be hard. When you speak out loud, any dragon nearby can hear you. If you want to limit who can hear, you need to visualize them when you're speaking. It can get complicated in a group setting, but for now, why don't you focus on me? For our purposes, that's all that matters. The others won't be back for a while. Just make sure not to say anything too incriminating about us or what we're planning."

How will you know if I'm only speaking to you or to everyone? Peter asked.

Because I'll tell you to shut up if I hear you, Blaze said flatly. *Seriously, Sana?*

He's working on it, I said. *The more dragons we have, the stronger we'll be. If we're to face off against the Hunters' Guild and the Master Guardian, we'll want all the help we can get.*

You're right, but that doesn't mean I have to like it. Try to get it under wraps soon so we can get some sleep. Sparky needs time to recover.

I chuckled out loud and looked at Peter. He'd lifted his head a little, but I could tell from his body language that he still wasn't over his embarrassment.

"It's okay, Peter. You're still learning. And to be honest, Sam doesn't know how to put a filter on yet, either. He screams into the void every time he talks."

Peter chuckled. In his dragon form, it came out something like a chirp. A puff of steam rolled out from between his lips, and he clamped his mouth shut.

"Give it another try," I said. I stepped forward and laid my hand on his snout. It was dangerous to stand so close to a new dragon in my human form, but I trusted Peter. He was still learning the ropes, but I figured it wouldn't be long before he had himself completely under control. I needed to show him that I believed in him—support was important, especially since he needed to learn so fast. If I gave him the impression that I was afraid he couldn't perform, it would only stunt his learning. "You've got this. Imagine me in your mind's eye as you speak. Just me. You've got this."

I don't know if I have it or not. It's complicated.

Both of us were silent for a moment, waiting for Blaze to chime in. He was silent.

"You did it," I whispered, pushing my cheek against the scales near his mouth. I heard the breaths he took and felt the warmth of his body, and it drew me to him even more. "Do it again. You've got this."

It's not hard to keep you in mind when you're so damned hot, Sana. Blaze, on the other hand...

Still no reply. I grinned. If Blaze had heard that, he *definitely* would have commented.

"Looks like you've got it down pat," I said. "You'll only need to communicate with me when we infiltrate the base, so why don't we work on broadening that filter to multiple recipients later? Right now, this is all you need."

What about fire lessons? Peter asked. *I'm going to need those to burn down the compound.*

"I'm pretty sure you'll be more efficient at burning down the compound if you *didn't* have fire lessons," I said with a laugh.

Why?

"Because if you learn to inhibit your fire, you're going to be way less destructive than a dragon who hasn't learned to hold it back. We need maximum damage as quickly as we can get it. I'm not going to teach you to restrict your fire only to have you pull back those barriers so you can torch a place to the ground."

Another puff of steam rolled from between Peter's lips. I stepped to the side to avoid it.

Sorry.

"No, you're fine." I kissed him, his scales smooth against my lips. "Do you want to try changing back? We'll need all our strength for tomorrow, and that means rest."

Can it also mean hours of sex? You know... to relax us, so we can sleep better. After what we just went through, I think we need to unwind.

"Are you going to fight me for it?"

If you want me to. But just know that it's your ass on the line, and I'm not intending to lose.

I grinned. "And I'm not going to give it up without a fight. I hope you realize that."

Oh, I do. Peter shifted back to his human form easily. My

heart swelled with pride. He'd learned so quickly. "I was hoping you'd say that. You should know by now that I like a little bit of struggle. What's life without a challenge?"

"Complacent," I said, grinning. I slipped my hand into his and led him back to his clothes.

"And complacency is the enemy of growth. So yeah, I'm ready for a fight." He dressed, then we headed back to the motel hand in hand.

Neither of us proved complacent. We both ended up winning that night, and took each other's bodies as our prize.

21

SANA

We saw my brothers-at-arms off the next day. Blaze carried Sam and the small omega that was trapped in stasis, both whom were strapped to his neck with the harness Peter had recently used to secure himself to me. Cory carried Brick, keeping his stiff form tucked against his underbelly. Peter and I stood to the side of the clearing while they took off, watching to make sure they were safe until they disappeared on the horizon. With Cory's cloaking ability and Sam's device in the pouch on each of their arms, I knew they'd be safe.

When we were alone, I rolled my shoulders back and glanced in Peter's direction. Peter's eyes were still on the skies, but now he looked in the direction of Sampson Mountain.

"How much time do you think we should give them to make sure they're really gone?" he asked.

"At least an hour. If there are any complications, they'll turn back before then."

"Sounds like a decent plan." Peter looked at me, a wicked grin stretching his lips. "Have I told you lately how wonderful your brain is? You set us up perfectly. I'm really impressed."

"I'm a cartographer's son," I said. "From the time I was young enough to lift a pen, I've been mapping out anything and everything. There's a lot of foresight required when you're making a map... I find it no surprise that I'm able to bring that kind of attention to detail to tactical planning."

"It's hot as hell, even if it's frustrating to try to talk you out of something." Peter grinned. "But this should be easy. We go in, we set shit on fire, and we get out. Nothing to it. If they're smart, they'll already have abandoned the base."

"We'll see." I didn't think it would be that easy, but Peter was the expert. As a former hunter, he had insights into the organization that I didn't have. I trusted him.

"What do you want to do with the hour we'll be waiting?" Peter asked, waggling an eyebrow.

I elbowed him in the ribs. "Forget it. We're going to need all our energy for the mission. We're not having sex right now."

"Spoilsport," Peter said with a laugh. "Well, I guess we'd better go rest, then. You up for a totally consensual, non-erotic nap?"

"Sounds great." I smiled at him, then bumped his shoulder with my own and headed back to the motel.

For as much as I wished the call of his heartsong had waited until I was finished making sure the royal family was safe, I was glad to have him at my side. Peter had given me a new take on life, and for the first time since I'd been appointed as one of Cory's men-at-arms, I found that I wasn't only working for the good of others... I was working for my own benefit, too. The sooner I made sure that Cory was safe and that the Hunters' Guild was decommissioned for good, the sooner I could enjoy having a family with Peter.

I'd never imagined that I'd find a happy ending of my own... but it had found me, and it was time that I took the steps necessary to make sure I could appreciate it fully.

WE FLEW BY TWILIGHT, hoping that the setting sun would blind any nearby hikers or motorists so they'd fail to see our dragons. It wasn't far to the Alpine Compound, but with Peter still so new to his body, we took our time. By the time we approached the mouth of the cave, the sun had set, and the world was plunged in shadows. All we had to go on were the reflective strips and LED lights put in place for helicopter pilots to reference.

We're going to fly straight to the building, I told Peter as we approached. *We're going to torch the whole thing from the outside. When I tell you it's time to go, we're going to get the hell out. Got it?*

And if the hunters come out?

They won't bother us. Our scales will protect us from their weapons, even if they shoot at us. If their defenses are anything like they were at the Pacific Compound, then we have nothing to worry about.

What about the potential for other dragons?

You said there was only one captive omega, didn't you? They'll need a captive alpha or an omega if they want to use a dragon against us. If that does happen, then we retreat. As long as we can get the dragon to a secluded place, I'm confident we can subdue it. Without a unicorn festival to work around, and with Cory so far removed from the area, I can attack as I was trained to. The fight only lasted so long before because we were under instruction not to kill the omega, and we had innocent lives to try to protect.

Peter's affection for me flooded the connection between us, and I returned it with my own.

You're a good warrior, Sana, he said. *I hope that Cory recognizes that.*

He's been very forthcoming with his praise in the past. After this stunt, however, I'm not so sure he'll be eager to recognize me for what I'm doing right now. I'm going against his word.

For good reason.

Sometimes, good reason isn't— We soared through the mouth of the cave right then... or at least, we tried to. A stunning jolt rushed through my body, and my wings buckled like I'd been crushed beneath a three-ton weight. With a chest-rattling roar, I hit the cavern floor hard. Less than a second later, I heard another thump as Peter hit the ground next to me.

I couldn't move.

To my horror, my dragon form started to slip away. The transformation was gradual, but no matter how hard I tried, I couldn't stop it. I couldn't access my dragon at all. It was like I was a preteen again, eager for the challenges of adulthood, but not yet mature enough to tackle them.

"Peter," I gasped as soon as my mouth was able to form the words. "Peter, are you okay?"

"F-Fuck... what's going on?" Peter uttered. He sounded dazed.

"Can you move?"

"No!"

"Stay calm." The last thing we needed to do was panic. I knew that Peter was a warrior, and that he'd been trained by his people to serve his country, but the circumstances we'd found ourselves in were well beyond the ordinary. I tried to lift my head, but it was like my body had fallen asleep. No part of me wanted to stir, no matter how much I tried to make it.

How had the hunters of the Alpine Compound set up a trap like this in a day's time? The damage to the base had to be extensive, and the last I'd seen, it had been completely devoid of life. How had they flown in people without us seeing? And, more important, how had they known to set something like this up? Very few things could stun a dragon. Had they been conducting tests on the captive omega? No wonder his mind was so closed off to me.

"Well, well, well," a man said from nearby. I couldn't turn my head to look at him. All I could do was listen as he stepped over my body. Cold metal met my wrists, and I heard a click as a lock activated. "Looks like the saying is true—the perpetrator always returns to the scene of the crime."

"Don't you fucking touch him!" Peter growled. "I will *end* you!"

"Big threats from such a little man," our aggressor said with a laugh. "Are you sure you can follow them through? Because I've seen your personnel file, and I have to say that I'm not all that impressed."

"Peter?" I asked, trying my best to pay no attention to the man who was handcuffing me. "Do you know him?"

"No. Some low-level piece of hunter scum, if I had to guess," Peter grumbled. "He's nothing, Sana. Don't pay any attention to him."

The hunter moved to straddle Peter's body—I heard his footsteps, then the click of metal as he did the same thing to Peter that he'd done to me. "You've got to tell me... were you a spy for the dragons all this time, or did you only turncoat once you got your dick wet in one? Because I'm assuming, based on how that fucking disgusting piece of shit next to you gasped your name as soon as he could, that he's putting out for you."

"Shut the fuck up," Peter snarled.

"That's as good as a yes. So, you're a traitor *and* a dragon fucker. Oh, the Master Guardian is going to have so much fun with you. He doesn't appreciate traitors, you know. Don't think that your time in service as a hunter is going to save you."

"If you harm him, I will *kill* you." Peter wasn't the only one who could snarl. I summoned as much venom as I could so that the hunter would know that I was serious. No one was allowed to harm my mate. *No one.*

He laughed. "Right. Because I'm so afraid of a sack of shit that can't transform into the fearsome evil dragon he really is." He kicked me in the ribs, and all the air left my lungs at once. "The handcuffs I just put you in? They'll inhibit your transformation, just like the pulse field we set up around the mouth of the cave did. Don't even try to change—you'll pop your fucking hands off."

There were more footsteps, and before I could catch my breath, I was being hoisted from the ground. Peter was shouting, his vicious words lost to me—the rattling gulps of air I sucked into my lungs were too loud to let me hear them.

We were tugged farther into the cave, led by muscular hunters that I couldn't turn my head to see. The world passed by in a blur, and before I knew it, we'd entered the Alpine Compound.

I had a feeling that this time, we weren't going to get out so easily.

22

PETER

We were thrown to the floor in a large room on the top level of the base. Unable to brace ourselves for impact, we fell hard. I hit my head, and for a moment, I was sure I was going to black out. Instead, bile rose up my throat in response to the pain, and I had to struggle to keep myself from throwing up.

Beside me, Sana hissed in agony. I wished there was something I could do for him, but I couldn't even protect myself, let alone the one my heart urged me to make my own.

"Look at this," a familiar, digitally altered voice said. It sent a shiver down my spine. I'd only ever heard it in recordings, but I knew better than to mistake it—it was the Master Guardian, the man who'd stepped into power a little less than a year ago.

"Not only have I been brought one of the dragons threatening to take over the world, but I've been brought a traitor as well."

The bottom of a boot met the side of my head, crushing down until I screamed in agony. The pressure on my skull was intense, and my skin felt like it would split open.

"Who would have thought that an organization devoted to ensuring mankind's survival would be infiltrated by someone like you—scum who thinks that he can betray the men and women whose world he's lived in his whole life. Tell me, Peter, what's more vile than that?"

"Enslaving omegas who are barely adults to do your bidding!" I hissed between clenched teeth. "How dare you do that to someone! He's a living, sentient being! A *person!*"

"You know that's a lie, Peter." The boot crushed down harder, and I roared in pain. "No alpha or omega is really a person, are they? Every single one of them is a slumbering dragon—a weapon waiting to be used against humanity. If I don't capture every one of them, what do you think will happen?"

"There have been dragons for as long as there have been people!" Sana argued, his voice shrill with urgency. "When have we ever attacked you? When have we ever harmed you? No one is trying to weaponize the descendants of survivors from the war. All we want is to live a peaceful life."

"So does peace start with burning down an entire compound

ALPHA DECEIVED | 185

and murdering the innocent people inside?" the Master

Guardian asked. "Or maybe peace begins with the dismantle-
ment of a place made to study and assess the very real threat
of dragons on the world? Do you really think you're clever,
pretending to be the heroes? All of your goals are selfish. You
won't stop until you've got what you want, no matter the cost
to humanity."

"That's not true."

"If that's the case, you've done a terrible job of proving it."
The Master Guardian chuckled. Whatever voice-altering
device he was using made his laugh sound robotic. I understood his need for utmost privacy, but the stiff, disaffected
laughter creeped me the fuck out. He eased his foot off my
head, which should have been a relief, but instead only terrified me. I heard him walk the short distance to Sana, then
heard Sana's bloodcurdling scream of pain. I lashed out
against my restraints, but my body was still betraying me.
There was nothing I could do.

"Sana, it's going to be okay!" I told him. "Be strong. You can
get through this. You're tough."

"Maybe in dragon form, when he's not inhibited," the
Master Guardian said. "But like this? He doesn't stand any
better of a chance than you do. Even as the effects of the
pulse wear off, you won't be able to do anything to stop me.
The cuffs restraining you were built to withstand a dragon's

transformation. You're stuck. All you can do now is give in to me."

A squirming sensation started in my stomach—he was lying. Sensation returned slowly—I could wiggle my toes and move my arms. In the back of my mind, I saw the glimmer of my dragon's scales, but there was nothing I could do to bring it out. I didn't want to end up like those young dragons Sana had told me about—the ones who'd crushed themselves to death by transforming in a cave far too small for them. I didn't know for sure what he was lying about, and I didn't want to risk my body over it.

"So, now that you've got that out of your systems, perhaps you'll listen to what I have to say." The Master Guardian stepped away from Sana, which was a small relief, but when he circled around to me, I knew that he wasn't done yet. "There are still dragons out there—three of them who've woken up from ancient times, and then a few others who have awoken thanks to your meddling. There aren't many alphas and omegas in the world—several thousand, perhaps. We're monitoring them now, tracking their locations. Once we've captured the ancient dragons and neutralized them, one by one we'll collect the alphas, omegas, and their families, and put an end to this once and for all."

I could move now, and I turned my head to look at Sana. He

was squirming as well, fighting against his cuffs in an attempt to free himself. His jaw was clenched.

"But how, pray tell, do you kill a dragon?" the Master Guardian asked. He clucked his tongue thoughtfully. "Bullets won't work. Fire won't work, either. Interfering with their heartsongs through electromagnetic pulses seems to work—it stopped the two of you in your tracks, after all."

"How do you know all this?" I demanded. "Who's been feeding you information?"

"Why, the quietest of your group... the one who always listens, only to take what he hears and report back to me." The Master Guardian chuckled, and my blood ran cold. Beside me, Sana gasped.

"You're lying!" Sana cried. "Brick would never betray us! He's the most loyal of us all!"

"I agree. He has been exceptionally loyal to me." I heard the vicious grin on the Master Guardian's face, but I couldn't see it. His whole body was concealed beneath a heavy cloak, and his face was shrouded by a massive, sturdy hood. I tried to roll onto my back to give myself better leverage, but the Master Guardian was quick. He planted his foot on my head to pin me down, and I screamed in pain once more. "So, after consulting with Brick, I've come to this conclusion—only a dragon can kill a dragon."

The Master Guardian's foot shifted so that it pinned me by the jaw instead of by the temple. I felt him adjust his weight.

"No!" Sana screamed. His voice curled with terror. "STOP! You've already captured me! Use me instead! Use *me!*"

I had no idea what was going on, or why Sana sounded so terrified, but I struggled against the Master Guardian regardless. It only made matters worse. I figured out too late why Sana was screaming—something sharp and metallic broke the skin on my temple, and the Master Guardian wasted no time putting the full force of his weight behind it. The pain was agonizing, and I bellowed as the metal spike pierced my bone and sank into my skull. The same kind of mind-control device I'd pulled out of the captive omega was now embedded in my body, and there was nothing I could do to stop it. My vision frayed at the seams, and thoughts left my head.

Then there was nothing. So much nothing.

I was gone.

Only the Master Guardian remained.

23

SANA

*N*o sound I could make could properly express my terror, and no words I could say would properly encapsulate how I felt as the Master Guardian drove the metal spike into Peter's temple. I struggled against my body and the metal cuffs keeping my arms in place, knowing that if I tried to access my dragon, I'd only end up hurting myself.

"Stop!" I pleaded, knowing that it was already too late. "Take me instead. He doesn't deserve this! You have me! Use me against my friends, not him!"

The Master Guardian drew back from Peter's convulsing body. He paid no attention to what I had to say. Instead, he took a handheld device from the pocket of his cloak and turned a knob. Peter's body went still, and I sobbed in fear and defeat. I'd managed to undo the damage dealt to the captive omega, but as far as I knew, he was still in stasis. How long would Peter be taken from me if I could turn the tables and get him back? Would he ever wake up?

Wings emerged from Peter's back clumsily—his shoulder blades were pinched together since his wrists were cuffed, and his wings brushed against each other as a result. Slowly, he began to transform.

"No. No, please, stop this!" I begged. The cuffs would dig into his arms so deeply that they'd cut important arteries. Peter would die from blood loss. "Have you no compassion? What has he ever done to you? He's only here because he loves me. He's never hurt anyone. Take me! Take me instead!"

The Master Guardian didn't react to my plea. The transformation didn't stop. I watched in horror as Peter's body started to grow... then narrowed my eyes as I heard the telltale creak of metal bending out of shape.

As his body expanded, his handcuffs warped and stretched, then broke. I blinked in surprise and realized that I'd been tricked—the Master Guardian might have set up a trap by the mouth of the cave, anticipating our arrival, but he had no containment devices ready. I wouldn't hurt myself during my transformation any more than Peter had, and that meant that I had a chance.

With a startled cry, I woke the dragon in my soul and begged him to come to the surface. With enough training, the sluggish, comfortable transformation between man and dragon could be shortened. It meant pain—the soothing numbness the dragon brought with it wouldn't have time to take effect— but in this case, it was necessary. I tore the dragon from his slumber and let myself succumb to the beast within.

My bones broke and reformed. My muscles stretched to accommodate them, as did my skin. I screamed until my vocal cords dissolved, and even after that, I fought the pain inside. But then, I heard metal twist and break. My arms were free, and as the dragon took control, I lumbered to my feet and faced my now fully transformed mate. He was just getting through his transformation, and he shook himself from head to foot as if he was damp from the rain.

I didn't see his soul in his eyes, and our heartsong had gone silent. I'd never felt so horribly before—not even after being woken by Sam's fake heartsong all that time ago.

Peter, I pleaded with him. *Peter, come back to me. It's Sana, your mate, and the father of your unborn child. Don't let him win. We can't let him win!*

Flames licked free from Peter's lips, and I recoiled. It wasn't Peter anymore, I realized. As long as the device was implanted in his head, the Master Guardian was in control. I needed to get the device out of him before it caused Peter to do something he'd regret. There was no time to keep my distance—I needed to act now.

I rushed at Peter before he could get the upper hand, prepared to knock him to the ground and swipe the metal device from his temple. Before I could, Peter reared up and snagged me, and we toppled to the ground together. His drag-onfire scorched my scales, and I hissed in pain, but perse-vered. We grappled hand to hand, his claws sinking into me. The searing pain of each razor-sharp claw as they pierced my scales and sank into my skin was intense, but I couldn't let it get to me. I tore away from him and swiped at his head, but Peter ducked. We tumbled again, struggling for dominance.

Peter, I begged him as we fought. *Please come back to me. I need you. You can fight this.*

Peter didn't respond, and the heartsong didn't return. It was like I was fighting an empty shell—and in a way, I supposed I was. I had no idea what the device in his head did, but it had robbed him from me, and I had no clue if I'd ever get him back.

The clear secondary eyelid that shielded my eyes from the wind while flying and allowed me to see without disruption while underwater blinked away tears, and I let the anger and sorrow in my soul out all at once in a lung-crushing roar. I pinned Peter to the ground and tore at the metal device.

It skittered across the floor, leaving a bloody trail in its wake. Dark blood oozed from Peter's temple, and his vacant eyes flooded with spirit for just a moment before he wilted. The heartsong returned, but his body fell. I roared again, the sound choked with sorrow, and collapsed next to my fallen mate.

Peter? I asked, nuzzling him with my snout. *Peter... please. Please answer me. I need to know that you're okay.*

As I made contact, I funneled my energy into him in an attempt to reverse the damage done. The captive omega had gone into stasis after the removal of his device, but I had no idea how long it had been inside of him, polluting his body and his mind. Peter had only been under its influence for a handful of minutes. There was a chance he'd be okay.

Slowly, his body began to repair itself. The bleeding stopped. The wound in his head knitted itself closed. I draped my wing over him and mourned him, even though I knew he wasn't gone. This was all my fault.

No.

It was the fault of the Master Guardian. He was the one who'd done all this—who'd put our lives in danger and injured my mate.

He would suffer for what he'd done.

I scrambled to my feet to find the Master Guardian was on the move, heading to a door on the far side of the room. The men who'd brought us into the room were gone—whether they'd fled or been dismissed, I didn't know. Frankly, I didn't care. At that moment, my only goal was to get to the Master Guardian and stop him.

I wouldn't let him harm Peter or anyone else again.

My agility as a dragon bested his speed as a human, and I cleared the room before he could make it to the door. A slash of my claws shredded the cloak he wore and cut into his skin, soaking the fabric in blood. Pieces of it fell to the floor, but I paid them no heed. I didn't try to claw at the Master Guardian again. I was too stunned to act.

I couldn't believe what I was seeing.

Blond hair. A wizened face. A slender frame.

Orris, Cory's advisor and trusted mentor, looked at me with his stony gaze. The Master Guardian, leader of the Hunters' Guild, was an ancient dragon—our long-lost former ally.

He'd been trying to kill us all.

24

SANA

O rris? I asked in disbelief, unable to take my eyes off
him. I scanned his temple for a device, but saw
nothing. His eyes still flickered with life, and as far as I could
tell, he looked like the same man I'd known from so long ago—
no one was controlling him. What he did, he did of his own
volition. *What is the meaning of this? What—*

Before I could finish my sentence, pain ripped through my
body, originating in my shoulder blades. I stifled a cry and
swung my head around to look at what was happening. My
wings, once proud and strong, were starting to curl from age
like desiccated leaves. They grew older at such a rapid rate
that I was sure, before long, they'd dry out and turn to dust.
Before that could happen, I started to transform back into my
human form.

Orris had never used his draconian gifts against me before, but now I knew his might. I never wanted to feel pain like that again.

"You should have let him kill you, Sana," Orris said. His voice was changed, but I wasn't sure how. There had to be some kind of hidden technology sewn into the front of his cloak, or possibly the neck of his shirt. "It would have been easier that way."

"What are you saying? Who's making you do these things, Orris? The rest of us have awoken. We can save you. You don't need to listen to whoever is threatening you anymore— we can fight for you."

"I always considered you the smartest of the group, but it seems that you're still nothing more than a fool." Orris shook his head slowly. "No one is controlling me. No one is telling me to do anything at all. I've made this organization my own, and I've shaped it to my will. The men here? They're under my command. I'm in control, and I rule an army... a kingdom."

My blood chilled. "What are you saying?"

"I will be the only one of the ancients left," Orris said. His voice was cold, like he considered me an inferior creature he wanted to exterminate, not an old friend who'd taken counsel from him on more than one occasion. "The age of dragons is over not because draconians were weak, but because they grew too complacent. We went from being feared apex predators, kings of the universe, to doughy, softhearted creatures who cared far too much about the comfort of other races. It shouldn't have surprised anyone that war broke out like it did. We are a race of warriors—of strong, capable individuals with strict hierarchies."

"That's not true."

Orris looked at me with disgust. "Of course you would think that. I told Coryphaeus not to bring you on—that doing so would be an affront to the sanctity of the royal family. An omega has no place standing in as a dragon warrior to the Crown Prince—not even one who looks and behaves like an alpha."

The hairs on the back of my neck stood up. "What?"

"You are a representation of everything wrong with the way draconian society went," Orris said, voice as cold as ever. "Traditions are traditions for a reason—they've proven themselves to work. Bringing an omega onto the team? Asking him to protect the life of someone so important?" He scoffed. "It's an affront against what we stood for as a society... and I will never have it happen again."

Something in me changed when he said that. It knocked the wind from my lungs and made me want to drop to the ground and curl into myself from pain. I staggered backward, my eyes ever on Orris. Was he aging my lungs? My heart? My mind?

When I could take no more and doubled over in pain, I knew. My once-flat stomach was bulging—rounding.

Orris was targeting my unborn child.

"Orris!" I cried. "Stop!"

"If you weren't an omega, this wouldn't have happened to you," Orris said calmly. Pain pulsed through my body and I screamed, clutching at my heavily pregnant stomach. "This is why omegas can't be warriors. This is why Coryphaeus never should have brought you on. Do you see why you're inferior? Do you feel it in your bones? In your muscles? In your flesh?"

The pain was too intense to speak. I let loose with another scream of agony, then collapsed to my knees. Slick rushed down my bare thighs, and I smelled blood.

If he killed my baby, I would kill him. I would tear each of his limbs from his body like petals from a flower, and I would use my gifts to make sure he stayed conscious through it all. I would tear him open and force him the feel the same pain he was causing me. His death would not be quick, nor would it be pleasant.

He'd taken everything from me. Everything.

"You opened your legs for an alpha—a traitor to your own

kind. You brought the enemy to bed and fucked him, Sana. You let him take your heat again and again, didn't you? You reveled in the attention. You put your own pleasure before the safety of the Crown Prince."

"Stop!" My voice was barely intelligible. Tears streamed down my face, hot and fat. The pain grew, and I collapsed onto my side, clutching my belly like it might save the life Orris was trying to rob me of.

"You are nothing more than breeding stock," Orris hissed through clenched teeth. He stood over me, his face twisted with rage I couldn't comprehend. "A whore all of us should have used for our own pleasure—not trusted as a brother. Do you think you can stand your own against an alpha? Do you really think that you can conquer your birthright and rise above? It's because of people like you that the draconian race fell... and weak leaders like Coryphaeus only made it worse. When I kill him, order will be restored. The draconian descendants who don't bow to my will and embrace my reign over the human race will die, just like you will."

More slick rushed down my thighs, soaking me, and a series of sharp pains spiked through my abdomen. I screamed and clutched at my stomach, but I knew it was a lost cause. The slick, the blood, the pain... I was about to deliver. Orris had sped my pregnancy along the full nine months, and my child was ready to be born.

"The draconian race will rise again," Orris said. "I will lead them, and whoever stands in my way will be destroyed. There is no room for men like you in our new world, Sana... and when Coryphaeus falls, and the rest of the dragon warriors make their choice, no one will be left to oppose me."

"Except for me, you fucking bastard," Peter snarled. I was sure that I'd imagined his voice. He'd been on the floor, unconscious, until moments before. It had to be my imagination playing tricks on me.

I looked up just in time to see Peter in his human form, swinging a vicious right hook at the back of Orris' head. Before the punch could land, Orris' body flickered, then disappeared.

He was gone.

Peter launched himself to the floor beside me, seemingly not interested in where Orris had gone. He laid a hand on my swollen stomach, then looked at me, terrified. "Sana?"

"He can influence time," I uttered. "H-He targeted the baby..."

"Is our baby okay?"

"I don't know." Another contraction squeezed me from the inside, and I shrieked in pain. I'd attended several deliveries before—my draconian gift meant that I was often requested in Novis to assist with troubled pregnancies—and I knew that pain like this wasn't standard. Something was wrong—probably whatever evils Orris had done to my body, and the body of my unborn child.

"What can I do?" Peter asked.

I squeezed my eyes shut and fought off a fresh round of pain. "Y-You need to deliver the baby. I can't reach with my claws, or else I'd do it myself."

"With my *claws?*" Peter asked, floored. "You want me to cut you open so that I can—"

"Please!" I didn't mean to scream it, but the pain had come on so suddenly that I couldn't do anything but. "Something is wrong. You need to help me. Please, Peter. I *need* you."

"I..." Peter swallowed. "I'll do the best that I can."

I knew he would. At this point, all I could hope was that it would be enough.

25

PETER

I had no idea how to summon my claws, so I woke the dragon inside and waited for my body to go numb. As my wings grew from my back, I watched my hands, silently willing my claws into existence. The precision an incision like Sana was asking me to make would require me to remain human—as a dragon, I was too large and lumbering to hope for that kind of accuracy.

"You need to try to be still," I told Sana, trying my best to be delicate. My fingernails reshaped themselves into black claws, and I tried to dissociate myself from the dragon to stop the transformation from progressing any further. It was tricky, and I had great respect for the dragon warriors who slipped in and out of partially transformed states so easily. "Can you lie on your back for me?"

Sana rolled onto his back. He was breathing hard, and his muscles tensed every time a new contraction hit.

"All you need to do is make the incision and remove our child," Sana said through his pain. I had no idea how he could be so levelheaded at a time like this. If I were in his shoes, I'd be a mess. "Once the baby is safe, I'll repair the wound. I just... I need help getting it out. Please, Peter."

"I'm ready," I said. The claws I'd grown were small and short, but they were wickedly sharp. "Are you ready?"

"Yes," Sana said through a groan. "Do it."

I sucked in a breath, prepared myself for what was to come, then sliced into the stretched skin of the man who made my heart sing.

Sana screamed, but he didn't thrash or roll away from me. I followed the underside of his belly, amazed at how easily his skin broke when it met my claw. When the wound was large enough, I got rid of my claws and wings, then reached in and grasped the tiny body I found inside.

"That's it," Sana said. He was crying, but he held himself together enough that he could still direct me. Even when he was at his weakest, he was strong. "Keep going."

The only thing left to do was pull our child from his body. I closed my eyes and pulled my hands back, and with a wet noise, I delivered our child.

I took care with removing the placenta, its cord still attached to our child's small body. With a mental shrug, I let the rest of the afterbirth fall to the floor while I focused on the cord. Drawing from the memory of a native's field birth I'd seen back in my military days, I bent over and laid the child on the floor. Pinching the cord with one hand, I did my best to summon a single claw. When it appeared, I used it to slice the cord and free him. I allowed the excess to fall to the side while I deftly tied a knot by where the boy's navel would be. If memory served, the end would dry and fall off as the navel healed.

I focused on retracting my sharp claw, then scooped the little guy back into the curve of my arm.

Sana sucked in a breath. His hands pressed against the site of the injury. His gift allowed him to close it to stop the bleeding, and he busied himself with making sure he was put back in one piece. I knew that I should have helped him, but I was too busy staring at the tiny human who was now in my arms.

Our son.

He was small—almost too small to be real—and his skin was wrinkled and red. I didn't have any clothes to clean him with or wrap him in, so I did the best job I could cleaning him with tender strokes of my thumb, then held him to my chest. His bitty hands grabbed at my skin, looking for something to cling to, and I rocked him slowly as he opened his mouth and let loose with his first wail.

"It's a boy," I told Sana. "He's... he looks healthy. I don't know how to tell if he really is."

Sana was cleaning himself up, and I noticed the wound I'd made on his abdomen stitching itself closed. It started to shrink—the blood left on his skin the only sign of what I'd done.

"He's crying," Sana said softly. His voice shook. "That's... that's what matters right now. Do you have anything to wrap him in?"

"No." I looked around the room. There wasn't anything there, either. "There's nothing."

"Then we'll need to be careful to keep him warm. Somehow, we'll have to get him off the mountain."

I had no idea if the mouth of the cavern was still trapped or not, or if the compound was staffed or empty. We'd been left alone, miraculously enough, which made me think that Orris had evacuated the hunters who'd brought us in as soon as he could. As confident as he was that he couldn't be defeated, no human wanted to mess with two adult dragons—especially not when those dragons were defending their young.

"We need to burn this place down," I said. I held our son, still in awe that he was real. "Do you want to take care of that, or do you want me to do it?"

"Together..." Sana said, voice strained. His wound was gone, and although he was pale, he seemed as determined as ever. He held out his arms. "If you give him to me, I'll keep him safe."

I looked him over, trying to get a sense for if he was well enough to do it. I didn't want him exerting himself, especially if he was adamant that he'd be the one to care for our boy. All of it was unbelievable. We'd only just been getting to know each other, and now here we were... parents. We hadn't even had time to discuss names.

I trusted Sana, and I felt confident that his word was true. Gingerly, I handed him our newborn son. Sana held him to his chest, closed his eyes, and held him for a prolonged moment. Then, pushing past his lingering pain, he slowly rose to his feet. Our son had stopped crying.

"Are you ready?" Sana asked.

"I am," I said with a nod of my head.

Sana met my gaze and smiled. "Then let's burn this place to the ground and get the hell out of here."

26

SANA

*A*s the Alpine Compound burned behind us, we flew. I scorched the previously unseen electronics that lined the mouth of the cave with a blast of my dragonfire, and we jetted out of the cave unharmed. It was night now, and the wind was bitterly cold, but I kept our son safe from the harsh winds and low temperatures. He was cradled in my hands, cupped against my chest closest to where my dragonfire burned. The scales there were always warm, and although it wasn't the best way to care for a newborn, it was all I could do. We didn't have far to fly, anyway, and once we landed and reclaimed our clothing, we could swaddle him to keep him from being too cold.

In the past, I'd been told that Orris' abilities were only temporary—that if he manipulated a person to increase or regress their age that the effects would be reversed before long. I had a feeling that he'd either been lying to us all this time, or that his power had grown since we'd last been part of the same team. Whatever the case, what we'd learned today was troubling. As soon as we landed and cared for our son, I needed to talk to Peter about it. With his lie detector ability, he'd be able to know if what Orris said was true or not... as long as he'd heard it firsthand. I had no idea if he'd been conscious for long enough to hear some of what had been said.

We landed in the small clearing behind the motel and changed back to our human forms. I kept our son tucked against my chest, careful to take my transformation slowly so that no harm came to him. Peter was not nearly as graceful, and his body twisted as he became human once more.

As soon as Peter was finished, he raced to my side and laid a hand on my back to support me. "Sana, are you okay? Is he okay?"

"We're fine." I smiled at him. "Can you please get me my clothes? I'll wrap him in my shirt."

"Sure. Of course."

Peter rushed toward the pack we'd left by the base of one of the nearby trees and brought it to me. He opened it and pulled my shirt from inside. I took it from him and wrapped our son up, protecting him from the cool night air.

"You're okay to walk?" he asked. "I can... I can carry you."

I smirked. "You're acting awfully flustered. I guess you're cashing in now, since you couldn't when I went into labor? Is that it?"

"No," Peter denied.

"I don't need your lie detector gift to know you're full of shit."

Peter laughed. "Hey! That's not fair. I'm just looking out for the man who carried my child... even if he only had to do it for a few days."

"If anything, that makes the experience more intense. Cramming in nine months of work into a few days? I guess that means we're not going to have problems fitting years of work into..." I trailed off as realization dawned. I wouldn't have nine months to fit in years of work—not anymore. Orris hadn't managed to kill me, but he had cut my time as a guardian short. When Brick and Blaze found out...

Peter rubbed my back reassuringly. "It's going to be okay."

"How is it going to be okay?" I asked. "I can't pretend he isn't my son—I won't let myself deny a life I made. When they find out, it's going to be just like Orris said... they're going to think I'm not capable. No omega should be allowed to protect the royal family. We're too vulnerable."

"You don't believe that."

210 | SUSI HAWKE & PIPER SCOTT

"No, but they do." I let out a sigh. There was a lot to think about and a lot to adjust to, now that life had taken such an unexpected turn. Was I ready to be a father? When I looked down at my son's face, my heart said yes—so why was it that my mind was telling me no?

"I don't know, Sana... I think that you're not giving them enough credit. I don't know Brick very well, but I know that Sammy would never take to someone who didn't treat him with respect. Even if Blaze is a loudmouth sometimes, I don't think you have anything to worry about from him. You're his friend, and you have been for... well... thousands of years, right?"

I looked at him, trying to find a fault with his reasoning. I couldn't find any. "Yes."

"So he's going to love you even after he finds out that you're an omega. You've served together for too long for him to turn his back on you now. You've more than proved your worth."

"How do you know that?" I asked, raising an eyebrow.

Peter shrugged. "I figured that it was true based off everything I've seen. The other dragon warriors respect you, and it's clear that Cory thinks very highly of you, too. That's not going to change."

I nodded, but found it hard to internally accept.

"Now, let's go inside and get you and the baby cleaned up. We're going to need to figure out what to do about him. We don't have any formula, do we? Babies that young don't eat baby food, right?"

I pinched my lips together to resist a sigh. For as nervous as I was now that I was a father, it looked like Peter had it a thousand times worse. He had a lot of learning to do, and he was going to have to do it on the fly.

"Let's go inside," I said. "We'll get all of this sorted out once we settle down. I don't know about you, but I'm exhausted, sweaty, and sore."

"I have a headache from hell," Peter chimed in.

I snorted. "I wonder why."

"But you know... it was worth it." Peter dug through the bag again and passed me my pants. He held the baby while I dressed, then passed him back to me so he could dress as well. "We still got done what we set out to do, and more than that... we learned things. Important things."

"Things I need to ask you about once we get settled," I said. "But for now, there are other things to worry about. Our son needs to come first. We may have a mission, but we're fathers now. I won't let one stand in the way of the other."

"Agreed."

Peter shouldered the pack and placed a hand on the small of my back, directing me forward while he walked at my side. I found myself leaning against him a little more than I should have, seeking support. He was there for me, even though I knew he had to be drained from the ordeal we'd just been through.

Less than a week ago, we'd been little more to each other than strangers. Now we were lovers and shared the responsibility of parenthood. I trusted Peter with my life, just as he trusted me with his.

It was a wonderful but frightening feeling to be so attached to someone so soon, but I couldn't help how I felt. The heart-song was my lie detector, and I knew that it always told the truth.

I was in love with Peter, and no matter what happened, I knew that as long as we had each other, we'd be happy.

PETER

*W*e cared for our son together. Sana took him immediately into the bathroom, and I heard the sound of water running down the drain of the sink. While he heated the water, I took care of things in the bedroom. We didn't have a crib, so I stripped the sheet from the bed and decided what the best course of action would be. At such a young age, I didn't think that our son would be doing much rolling around—but I knew as much about babies as I did about open-heart surgery, so I had no fucking idea if I was right or not.

I brought the sheet into the bathroom to find that Sana had our son cradled in one arm. He ran a wet washcloth over his skin, cleaning away the fluids we hadn't been able to take care of back in the Alpine Compound.

"Is this going to be okay?" I asked, showing Sana the sheet. "I figure that one of us could make a sling, and we can keep him cradled to our chest all night. We can either take shifts sitting up with him, or, if you trust me, I'll take responsibility for the whole night."

Sana looked me over, silently drawing conclusions. I saw the wheels turning behind his eyes. "You're the one who had the spike pushed through his skull."

"You're the one who went from a few days pregnant to delivering a fully grown baby over the course of a few seconds," I retorted. "I wasn't forced to nurture a child to maturity all in one go, then ripped open to have that child delivered."

Sana laughed. It was soft and airy, but behind it, I heard its truth—it was exhausted and nervous. He was still worried about what would happen to him when the others found out the truth.

"I'm still working on what we can feed him," I said. "I'm thinking that I can hitch a ride into town, or that maybe I can call for a taxi from the main office of the motel to take me to the nearest grocery store. I... well, to be honest, I'm not entirely sure what to buy, but I'm banking on finding a mother with children there who might be able to give me some advice. Maybe I can find a temporary crib while I'm out."

"We had wet nurses in Novis," Sana said. "Pregnant individuals would often band together, and the females would help the male omegas make sure their children had what they needed. I'm not sure if you'll find a wet nurse available in the grocery store, but you can certainly ask one of the mothers there if we can purchase her assistance."

I choked back a laugh. Sana looked up from our son, a quizzical expression on his face.

"What?" he asked.

"You obviously haven't been paying much attention to how Cory and Emery have been raising Cora... or how Sammy and Blaze have been raising Sophia and Tidus. There aren't wet nurses now. At least, not that I know of. Maybe the very rich have them, but, uh, that's not us. At least, not unless we can tap into some of Sammy's money."

"Then what do children eat?" Sana asked, blinking in confusion.

"Formula or some shit." I laughed. "I have no idea. I've been a dad for what, all of an hour? Maybe two? I wasn't exactly prepared to be one for another nine months, so you kind of caught me with my pants down."

"An hour ago, we were burning an enemy base to the ground. Now, we're cleansing our newborn and wondering how we're going to be parents when we know nothing. Is this real life?"

"It's as real as it gets." I kissed him on the cheek. There was a mirror in front of the sink, and in it, I saw our reflections. We were an unlikely pair, but damn, did we look good together. And to see the life that I had helped create now in Sana's arms? There was no better feeling than that. "I'll go into town and get him some basic supplies. Since I'm more familiar with this time period than you, it's our best bet. I'll need you to stay here with him and hold down the fort. I'll set you up with the sling before I go."

"Do you think he's going to be a good baby?" Sana asked. His voice was quiet and filled with wonder. "I... never had a chance to know him when he was inside of me. I never had the time to dream about his personality, or what his likes or dislikes might be. I didn't even have a chance to fantasize about what kind of gift he might receive—something to do with blood, like my family, or something to do with detecting the truth, like yours."

"Maybe he'll surprise us by being a wildcard." I winked, then left his side to prepare to leave. The last thing I wanted to do was leave my newborn and his father, but I had responsibilities now. Sana was strong and capable not only in battle, but in emotional matters. He would take care of things just fine. "While I'm gone, maybe you should start thinking up names. I know we didn't really have a chance to discuss it beforehand, so we're going to have to make a split-second decision."

"We'll know the right name when it comes to us," Sana said. He turned off the water and stopped me before I could leave the bathroom, claiming my lips in a lingering kiss that made me want to take him straight to bed not so that I could fuck him, but so that we could make love. I'd made a baby with this man—our hearts and our lives were tied together in immeasurable ways. I wanted him more than I could remember wanting anyone else, physically and emotionally.

The kiss broke and I took a half-step back. My head was swimming with love for him, and had it not been for our son's needs, I would have stayed. I wrapped the sheet over his shoulder and knotted it so that he'd have a sling to hold our son with while I was gone. "I'll be back as soon as I can."

"Here." Sana squeezed a washcloth he'd been soaking in the sink and tossed it at me. "There's still blood on your face. At least wipe that up before you go. You don't want to scare the mothers in the grocery store before you can even ask for their help, warrior."

Warrior? My lips twitched upward just for a moment. It was a great honor to be referred to as an equal by a man strong enough that he'd been asked to protect the royal family. Slowly, I was finding my way into their group and making a name for myself. I was an outsider no longer.

I washed up quickly, tossed the bloody rag into the tub, then winked at Sana and headed out of the bathroom. Before he was out of my sight, Sana rolled his eyes and shook his head playfully.

Love wasn't what I'd imagined it would be—somehow, it was better.

I left our motel room and started to find my way to the grocery store. There was still something I needed to tell him, but it could wait. Right now, we needed to focus on the new life we'd created. I wouldn't let anything ruin the small joy we'd found in our new family. In this dark time, we had to cling to hope—for just a little while longer, I'd gift Sana with ignorance. What I knew could wait. Our son would always take priority.

THAT NIGHT, after our son was cleaned, fed, and laid down to sleep in the portable bassinet I'd found while out in town, I took Sana to bed and held him in my arms. Both of us were naked, but too exhausted to search for pleasure in each other's bodies. We'd had one hell of a day, and I knew that we were only getting started.

"Back at the Alpine Compound, I saw the Master Guardian's face... he was Orris, our missing adviser," Sana told me in a whisper. He placed a kiss against my chest, over my heart. All night he'd been kissing and nuzzling there, and it soothed me like nothing else. "He's betrayed us."

"No surprise there. It's always the adviser that's evil, isn't it?" I asked.

Sana drew back to look at me in surprise. "What?"

I held back a laugh and stroked his hair. "Yeah, I guess you missed out on a *lot* of social media, what with you being frozen in time for thousands and thousands of years. It's, uh... well, it's kind of a thing. Like, have you ever seen *Aladdin*?"

"Who is 'Aladdin'?"

"Okay then, I'm going to take that as a no." I guided him back down to my chest, and he went back to kissing and nuzzling the spot over my heart that made me feel so good. "It's just... not a surprise. The adviser is always the evil one. But you know what? The adviser never wins, either. They'll get the upper hand, and they'll make you think there's no chance in hell that you're going to get out of whatever situation you're in, but you'll do it. The good guys always win. It's kind of the law of the universe... at least when it comes to movies."

"This isn't a movie," Sana said.

I shrugged. "I guess you're right, but I mean... it's good to have hope, isn't it? If you can't believe in your cause, then how can you see it through to the end? I believe that we can do this. I know it."

"Orris said that Brick had betrayed us," Sana told me. "If one of my brothers-at-arms is truly guilty of treason, then what hope do we have? We'll never know who to trust."

"Orris was lying. Brick is loyal," I said. I hadn't heard him speak the words, but I felt it in my gut—it was the same warm, squirmy feeling I got whenever I heard someone speak a lie.

"You heard him?"

"No." I grinned. "I think that maybe, my powers are growing. You said that's a thing, right? That as dragons get older, they get stronger? Maybe now that I'm in touch with my dragon, I'm figuring out new things about my gift that I never knew before."

"It's possible," Sana mused. "When young dragons transform for the first time, usually around the age of fourteen, their gifts bloom, too. Very few people reach adulthood without having transformed... but I assume that's what's happening now. I think you're right."

"I only know the bare bones of what happened today... but I know that Orris is committed to his plan. At least, the little I heard of it. But there's something I don't know... something that maybe you could help me with."

He stopped nuzzling the spot over my chest. "What is it?"

"I recovered something from the Alpine Compound," I said. I slid out from beneath him and reached for the pack we'd brought to the clearing. "A scrap of fabric."

"I'm not a tailor," Sana said. "I don't know the first thing about clothing."

"No," I admitted. I unzipped the small pocket on the pack I'd stowed it in and pulled it out. "But you do know about blood."

The pieces of Orris' cloak that had fallen during the fight were soaked in it. Sana looked at me, wide-eyed.

"You said that you can follow bloodlines, right?" I looked him in the eyes, hoping that my suspicion was right. "Can you follow his life backward through time if you have access to his blood? Can you see what happened since he woke up and parted ways from your group? Or maybe even how far back his deception goes?"

Sana replied breathlessly, "Yes."

"Then this might be the most important duty you've ever done for Cory," I said. I handed him the bloody cloth. "It's up to you, Sana. I only know surface-level truths, but you? You can go back and see what's really going on. I have faith in you." I grinned. "Let's take this motherfucker down."

28

SANA

$\mathcal{I}$ lifted the scrap of fabric to my lips and let my tongue come into contact with the blood. The signature belonged to Orris—I recognized it now just as clearly as I'd recognized it during our mission to the hoard. But now, I probed that signature, isolating the things that distinguished the blood from any other living being—things that only I could feel, see, and hear. I leaned into those threads, tracing them back, following their journey... and then, as the rest of the world bled away around me, a picture appeared before my eyes. It was something I'd never thought to look for—and something I wished I'd never had to see.

ORRIS, *weakened, stumbled as he pushed himself out from the* narrow slit of the cavern we'd taken shelter in all those years ago. He squinted against the harsh light and took a deep, inward breath, then laughed, and laughed, until his voice was hoarse and his throat was dry. He lurched forward and took to the forest, walking, seemingly unperturbed that he'd left all of us frozen in stasis and trapped in stone.

The scene changed. Orris sat in a room somewhere I didn't recognize. He sat across from a man dressed in a stiff uniform, small rectangular pins on the shoulders and breast of his jacket. They were having a conversation, I knew, but I couldn't hear the words. Orris had drowned them out, masking them from even his own memory.

The man was in the middle of a sentence when his face twisted with pain and fear. I watched as Orris drained the life from his body, aging him decades in a short span of time. He pushed further, and further, until the man's skin was stretched thin against his bone and his eyes were sunken into his head. He was left a husk, a skeleton with dried, thin skin. His strained, aged heart stopped. Orris plucked a placard from his desk—a name was inscribed upon it—and tossed it into the trash. Then, calmly, he stood and took the man's jacket. As the scene faded away, he slipped it on and adjusted it so it sat squarely on his shoulders.

There was a meeting with other official-looking men—an assembly with men I believed were hunters. His arrival at the

Alpine Base, the captive omega at his side, the spike already driven through his skull...

All of what I saw was what I already knew. Orris had betrayed us, and he was using the Hunters' Guild as a way to revert the world to how it had once been—to wipe our progressive king, Cory, out, and reintroduce the archaic conditions the draconian race had once abided by.

So I dug deeper.

I followed his history backward, to that time thousands of years ago when we'd entered the cave, convinced the enemy was still on our tail. As we huddled in the corner for protection, Orris stood behind us, the weakest and therefore the least accessible. I watched as he summoned magical strength from inside of himself, concentrating it until he could hold it no more. The resulting explosion of magic from his body detonated like a bomb, turning our bodies into elderly husks barely clinging to life. Stasis hit immediately, and at the same time, Brick's protective gift kicked in. It turned us all to stone, protecting our vulnerable flesh and keeping us rooted in place—nothing more than statues in a dark cave, out of sight and out of mind.

Orris was caught in the blast, too, and Brick's heart knew not of his betrayal. Orris was protected in stone—Brick's kindness had saved the life of the man who'd tried to kill us all.

But why?

I didn't understand why Orris hadn't tried to take over the world during the war, when draconian forces were divided, and when he could have recruited the dragons who had similar beliefs. I followed his history backward, searching for motive. I was exhausted, and I didn't know how many more years I could look back on before I was too tired to go on, but I knew I had to give this everything I had. Not only was Cory counting on me to figure this out, but my son was, too. I had too much to lose to give up.

A few days before we took flight for the last time, I watched as Orris cornered a young omega in an alley behind the inn we were staying at. I recognized the omega's blue eyes and lithe body, but it wasn't until I saw Orris push him face-first against the wall and tear his trousers from his body that I realized the connection. Orris forced himself onto the young omega as my heart broke and my stomach twisted into knots.

Emery's ancestry was dark. I wished I'd never seen the origin of his bloodline, but now I understood. His visions of events past, and Vivian's predictions of the future, were tied to Orris' gift of time. Orris had sired a child in his unwilling omega, and that line had survived the war and eventually borne my king's mate.

I looked back further yet. Orris sat in front of a small basin of water, gazing down into its surface. I watched as he predicted his own future—a nod to Vivian's power. Across the surface of the water, a scene unfolded. Orris did his best to rally support for his cause and defeat us, but in the end, he was slain. He wasn't strong enough to take on me and my brothers-at-arms, and he didn't have enough of a presence to rally the support he needed during a time of conflict.

"Then the solution is to wait until I am older and stronger," he muttered to himself, his lips twisting into a fiendish smirk. "As the years pass and my power grows, no one will be able to hold me back. The draconian race will tear itself to pieces, and I'll be there when it is long gone and forgotten to pick up the pieces and shape it into what it always should have been."

He poured the water out the window, set the empty basin down, and went to bed.

There was nothing more I needed to see.

I SNAPPED BACK to reality with a gasp. Peter was there to catch me. He wrapped his arms around me and guided me back down to the bed, whispering sweet words in my ear.

"You're fine, Sana," he murmured, doing his best to be reassuring. "You're here with me. I've got you. I don't know what you saw, but it can't hurt you here. I'm here to protect you. I'll *always* protect you."

I threw the bloody cloth to the side and swallowed the copper in my mouth. "Orris was the one who attacked Cory and the rest of us all those years ago, freezing us in that cavern. He... he's Emery's ancestor. They share the same bloodline."

"Shit," Peter murmured. He tugged me closer, tucking me against his chest. "A while ago, Sammy was telling me how strange it was that the enemy was able to infiltrate the apartment above Vivian's shop. He said that he'd triple-checked that it was configured to only let those who were part of the same family in... and I guess that explains why it malfunctioned. Emery must be distantly related to several other alphas and omegas... some of whom Orris had already swayed to his side."

"Thousands of years ago, he saw that he wouldn't be able to defeat us as he was. He... he put us all in stasis so that his power could grow, and so that the war would be over. Without other dragons to oppose him, and with his power heightened, he stands a chance at taking over the world."

"Too bad that fucker didn't anticipate that we'd be there to shut him down. We're going to stop him, Sana. I know it. Evil never wins."

"We can't do it alone." I breathed him in, trying to soothe myself with his scent. My stomach was still twisted into knots. "We're going to need the help of all the dragon warriors—every ounce of strength we have, we need to put toward shutting him down. He has the Hunters' Guild on his side, and the Central Compound is still active... and likely stronger than ever. He knows how to shut down our dragons and paralyze us. His powers are stronger now than they've ever been before..."

"But you know what?" Peter asked, determination building in his voice. "He's not the only one. Your powers are stronger, too. And now you have me and Sammy, Emery and Vivian, Nana... we may not be a mighty army, but we're strong in different ways. Our powers united will stop him, I know it."

"I hope you're right." I wanted to take comfort in what he said, but it was hard to do when I knew the odds were stacked against us. "If this doesn't go the way you think it will... some of us may not be coming out of this alive."

"Don't say that, Sana," Peter whispered. "We're going to make it. All of us are. We need to believe in ourselves and believe in each other."

"We need to see if they'll believe in me, first," I admitted with a tiny chuckle. I nuzzled against the place over Peter's heart where I longed to leave my mate mark. If we were to face death again so soon, I wanted to know that our bond was official. I closed my eyes. "We need to call someone to pick us up. We can't fly back as dragons when our son is so young. Do you think Sam will drive?"

"I'm sure he will... cursing us all the way." Peter snorted. "We'll explain what's happened to the others, introduce our son, then go on with our lives. No one is going to care that you're an omega, Sana. Do you think Brick and Blaze are like Orris? I don't believe that for a moment."

"We'll have to see," I said. "But, before that happens, before *anything* happens, I want to make things official with you, Peter. I want to promise you my heart and know that I have yours in return. Will you let me place my mate mark on you, and do the same for me?"

"Your mate mark?"

"How dragons pledge their love to each other," I told him. It was so strange to me that Peter was draconian, yet didn't know about mate marks. How strange the world had become. "It's how we tell our heartsong that we want to keep them forever... that our love will be theirs until the day we die."

"How do I do it?" Peter asked.

I stretched my neck to the side for him and traced a finger over the soft skin I wanted Peter to sink his teeth into. "All you need to do is bite me here, wherever it feels right to you. In exchange, I leave my mark on you over your heart."

"Mm, so that's why you keep kissing and nuzzling there. You've been begging me for my mark all night, and I've been too dense to know it."

My cheeks heated. "... Maybe."

Peter laughed. Then, without any warning, he pinned me to the bed and looked me right in the eyes. My heart raced, and the words he spoke didn't help it slow. "Of course I'll give you my mark, Sana. I would have given it to you on the very first day we met if only I'd known... and if only you hadn't resisted me so damned much."

"I had my reasons," I mumbled, my cheeks on fire.

Peter grinned. "I know you did, and I'm glad we got over them so quickly. I'll admit, it's weird to me that I could feel such powerful things for a man I've known for as short a time as I've known you, but... what we have, as strange as it is, is real, and I'm not going to let it go because it feels like it's too rushed or it's too soon."

He grazed his teeth against my neck, and I shivered in delight. Then, speaking against my skin in a low murmur, Peter spoke again. "I love you, Sana, and I'm going to make you mine. All mine."

He marked me, his teeth breaking my skin to prove to me that even when I was at my most vulnerable, I could trust him with my life. I gasped in pleasure and closed my eyes, letting the pain wash through me. The message it brought with it was too sweet to ignore: Peter was mine, and I was his. My heartsong would never leave. No matter what happened to me, I would always carry this happiness in my heart. I'd found a lover, a mate, and a family. Even in the darkest, most dangerous times, I'd found something to keep me going.

I hoped, as I sank my teeth into the spot I'd been worshiping over Peter's heart to leave my mark on him, that he felt the same way.

29

PETER

"quinn."

"No. Jackson."

"Who is Jack, and why are you saying our son belongs to him?" Sana frowned. He held our son against his chest, rocking him as he slept. "No. Lynis."

"No. Warren."

"No." Sana sighed. "We're not getting anywhere fast, are we?"

"Not really." I laughed. Sammy was supposed to be arriving within the hour, and we'd spent the day alternating between taking each other to bed and debating our son's name. "But at least we've got a long list of names we both agree that we don't want."

Sana sat on the edge of our motel bed. Our nameless newborn reached blindly for his chest and neck. Sana intercepted his tiny hands with a single finger, and our son latched on and squeezed.

"Well..." Sana said. "You said you were open to naming him a draconian name. Do you still feel that way, or are you going to shoot down all of my suggestions?"

"I'm open to it," I said. "But the name needs to be right. So far, none of the names you've suggested have been right for him."

Sana chuckled. He pulled his finger away. "What about Laurus?"

"Laurence?"

"No, Laurus. It sounds almost the same... perhaps it could be his English name." Sana smiled at our little bundle of joy. "It means achievement or victory. I feel like it's fitting."

I liked it. I settled on the bed beside Sana and leaned against him. "It feels right to me."

"And to me, too."

"Then Laurus it is." I kissed Sana's temple. "What a beautiful boy we've made together. I'm already so proud of him."

"With fathers like his, he's destined for greatness." Sana sneaked a bashful look in my direction. "I can only imagine the things he'll do, and how proud we'll be."

Before I could reply, there was a screech of tires in the parking lot. I laughed. "Looks like Sammy's here."

"I'll get Laurus settled into the car," Sana said. "I'd appreciate it if you could handle returning the keys to the front desk."

"You got it."

I rose, but before I left, I stole a look at Sana and Laurus. Sana was glowing—fatherhood suited him. I wondered if he saw the same glow in me.

I opened the door to our room a split second before Sammy knocked. His balled fist was raised, and his skinny body blocked the doorway. He yelped when he saw me and hopped back, but he didn't move to take cover. Instead, he held a hand over his heart and let out a frightened puff of breath. "You scared me."

"Sorry."

"I've come to bring you back home. I don't really understand why—" Sammy looked over my shoulder, and his eyes widened.

He took a step back, looked me over, then glared at me like the baby in the room was all my fault. Well, I supposed he *was* all my fault, but Sammy had no way of knowing that. "Peter?"

"Yes, oh dearest brother-of-my-heart?"

"Why the hell is there a baby in Sana's arms?"

"It's a long story," I said with a laugh. "It's a damned good thing that we have, oh, nineteen hours between here and home. I think we're going to need every second of it to tell you about everything that went on."

Sammy gave me a flat, disillusioned look, then shook his head and jerked his thumb over his shoulder at the navy-blue van left idling in the parking lot. "Then you'd better hurry up and get in. I'm planning to stop on the border of Utah and Nevada to rest only as long as it takes until I'm good to drive again, then we're back on the road. You'll need to condense your story so I can hear it all before I go to sleep tonight. It's going to make me worried, isn't it?"

"Very worried," Sana confirmed, brushing by me to step out of the motel room. He had the baby seat we'd bought Laurus in anticipation of our return trip home slung from his arm. "You may wish to seek my counsel afterward to treat your mental distress."

"He's... only slightly exaggerating," I admitted. Sammy's

shoulders sank. "But the good news is, we're both alive, and we're going to be stronger than ever. We've got this."

Sammy sighed. "Of course you do. Why wouldn't you?"

"Hey, have a little faith!" I laughed. "And, by the way, meet Laurus. Isn't he beautiful?"

"Whose baby is that?"

"Ours." I beamed. "It looks like we'll be raising our families at the same time, brother. Isn't that great?"

Sammy looked between me and Sana several times, lifted a hand like he was going to say something, then shook his head and dropped it again. "You have until the border of Utah and Nevada. There'd better be answers."

I laughed. "Of course there will be."

And after answers, there'd be action. That, more than anything else, was what I was eager for. We knew what Orris was up to, we knew the threats he posed, and we'd be ready. No matter what it took, I was determined to keep my family safe. An ancient dragon with a grudge wasn't going to get the best of me.

SAMMY DIDN'T SLEEP that night—at least, that's what I

assumed after I woke up and saw the dark bags under his eyes and the slight twitch that jolted through his body every now and then. I'd slept like the dead between alternating shifts with Sana to take care of Laurus, and miraculously felt totally rested, so I took over driving duties and let Sammy chill out in the back of the van with Sana.

"So he... he aged your days-old fetus in the span of a few seconds... and you delivered *immediately?*" Sammy asked, aghast. I was glad that he was in the back, because it meant I didn't have to hide my facial expressions. Even though I didn't laugh, my mirth sure as hell showed on my face. In the heat of the moment, what had happened had been terrifying, but in retrospect, it was nowhere near as scary.

"Yes," Sana said.

"And he... he killed a man by draining the life from him?" Sammy gulped. "He just... turned him into a skeleton, essentially?"

"Yes, but he was a human," Sana said. "As dragons, we have an advantage. With much longer lifespans, it won't take seconds to kill us. I know you're worried, but you don't have to be."

"Don't worry? Do you even hear what you're saying?" Sammy laughed desperately. I saw him rub his face through the rearview mirror. "There's so much to worry about that the only conceivable way I can see myself *not* worrying is if I forget about something while worrying about everything else."

"You'll be fine," Sana promised. "My brothers-at-arms and I will be there to protect you. We might need your help at some point, but you won't be asked to fight. Not in hand-to-hand combat, at least."

"That's not making me feel much better."

I held back a laugh and focused on the road. So far, the fact that Sana was an omega hadn't even been brought up. I was hopeful that the rest of the dragon warriors would treat the news the same way Sammy was—like it was no big deal.

"Well," Sammy said after a pause. "I'm glad that we know this now. If we went to take on the Central Compound blind, we would have been taken by surprise, and I'm willing to bet that would have spelled disaster for us. I enjoy not dying, so... thank you."

"You're welcome."

"You guys hungry?" I asked. We'd just passed a road sign advertising the restaurants at the upcoming exit. "There's an In-N-Out coming up."

"No, thank you," Sammy grumbled. "Let's keep it moving, gentlemen. We've got a lot of ground to cover, and lots to talk about when we get home. Unless it's an emergency, I don't want to stop... especially somewhere like that."

"You're the boss, Sammy." I rested my wrists on the top of the steering wheel and kept my eyes on the road ahead, enjoying this quiet moment. Soon enough, we'd be back in action.

Sana had been right—there was a chance we might not pull out of this one. If these were going to be some of my last moments alive, I wanted to cherish them. And with my ever-growing family by my side, that wouldn't be too hard to do.

I'd gone from a young man without any family at all to a man who'd found friends who'd stand by me no matter what. Sana, Laurus, Sammy, Nana, and the dragon warriors had given me a new lease on life. As a hunter, I'd been deceived and led astray, but they'd put me back on the right path.

I would never stray from it again.

EPILOGUE

SANA

The second the van was parked in the estate's luxurious garage, Sam scuttled off to go fortify the premises against attack. I remained seated on the back bench until Peter slid the door open.

"Do you want me to take Laurus?" he asked. "Or would you feel better holding him when we meet back up with the other dragons?"

"I'll take him," I said. "If I'm not holding him, they might not believe he's really mine. I've never had much to do with children before."

"I wonder why." Peter winked. He helped me out of my seat, then stood by as I unstrapped Laurus and held him to my chest. For some reason, the rough patches in the road had put him right to sleep. I supposed the rocking movement soothed him. Toward the end of the drive when he'd grown fussiest, Peter had gone out of his way to hit every pothole and rough spot to try to keep him asleep. Sam hadn't been much of a fan, but I think we all preferred being seasick over hours of screaming.

My brothers-at-arms had been waiting for us. They came through the door joining the house to the garage, but the joy on their faces disappeared when they saw I was holding a child. To my delight, Brick had woken from stasis and stood with the rest of them. He was the first who dared to speak. "Were there other captives, Sana? And babies, no less? Does the Master Guardian have no shame?"

"He's not a captive. Everyone... I'd like to introduce my son, Laurus."

Everyone was silent. Blaze, who'd come looking for Sam, no doubt, looked between me and Peter in total confusion. "Peter is an alpha, though. Unless... he's not. Was I wrong? I could have sworn I read his physical cues right."

"You did," I said. Fear condensed in my chest, but I knew I had to get it out. I couldn't hide the truth from them any longer. "I am, and always have been, an omega... and Peter is my heartsong, and now bears my mate mark."

I'd never seen so many blank expressions. An uncomfortable

silence passed, then Blaze laughed nervously. "That's a good joke, Sana. You guys must've been seriously bored to come up with something like that. So, who's the kid? You guys were supposed to camp at the motel until we came back to storm the Alpine Base together."

"This is our son," Peter said. He set a hand on my shoulder and squeezed. "That morning you teased us about being loud all night long? I was taking Sana's heat again, and again, and again."

I looked up at him, mildly embarrassed. "You don't need to be so specific. All it takes is one time to conceive. They don't need to know about how often we went at it."

"I know." Peter smirked. "But the look on Blaze's face is worth it."

Blaze looked equal parts disgusted and surprised, and I actually found it in me to laugh. Laurus stirred and gurgled, curling his hands in my shirt.

"Sana, is this true?" Brick asked. There was paternal concern in his voice, and it made me feel like there was a chance that my news wasn't going to be so ill-received after all. "You're an omega? How did we miss your heats? You look like an alpha."

"My body is the result of hard work," I said. "Where you, Blaze, and Cory were gifted your muscular bodies by birthright, I trained to develop mine. Cory asked me to be one of his guardians both because of the usefulness of my gift, and because I was physically able to hold my own against any naturally born alpha. He agreed to keep my secret to avoid complication. I used wasteweed regularly to stave off my heats and block out my omega scent. The effects of the wasteweed ran out over the last year after we woke in this new world, and after I met Peter, my heat manifested for perhaps the first time ever."

"And then he took your heat..." Brick glanced at Peter. "But I feel like there's no way the child could be yours. You've only known Peter for a short time. No child could have been born that fast..."

Now that I was sure that none of them were going to reject me for who I really was, I found the confidence to move onward like nothing had ever happened. The huge, life-changing news I was sure would ruin me turned out not to be all that bad after all.

"It's a long story," Peter said. "We should all move to the living room and get comfortable..."

"A long, frightening, terrible story," Sam called from elsewhere in the house.

Blaze perked up. "Sparky, there you are. I was looking for you. Instead, I found a mindfuck."

"And you're about to get mindfucked even more," Sam said as

he appeared in the doorway. "You *will* want to sit down for this one. It kept me up all night worrying."

"Then let's go take a seat," Cory said. "We'll hear what Sana and Peter have to say."

———

THE DRAGON WARRIORS listened in silence to our story, but I read their concern on their faces. By the time we'd shared all the details, the atmosphere in the room had changed. All of us had been deceived—we'd trusted a traitor, and what was worse, we'd cared for him.

"If it wasn't you telling me the news, Sana, I wouldn't have believed it," Cory admitted. "Orris... I thought that he was a curmudgeonly old man, stuck in his ways, but harmless. I never would have thought this..."

"I couldn't believe it, either," I admitted. "It was a low blow."

"Then what are we to do?" Brick asked. "We can't let him go on with his plan. He must be stopped. The world isn't ours anymore, and we have to accept that. All we want is to live in peace with the humans, but he... he wants to take control. He can't be allowed to do this."

"Perhaps the captive omega knows," Cory suggested. "I've been taking care of him since he returned. He's still in stasis, but I'm hoping that you might be able to do something for him, Sana."

"I can try," I said. "I healed him as best I could back in the Alpine Compound, but I'll admit that I was exhausted and under a lot of pressure. There is darkness in his mind... he's suffered psychologically at Orris' hands. I can try to ease some of that suffering, but I can't promise that I can fix anything."

"If you wouldn't mind trying, I'd appreciate it," Cory said. "He might know more about Orris' plans. You mentioned that many of his memories were blocked or muted. If the omega wakes up, he might be able to tell us what he's heard. Once we know what he has to say, we'll be able to make our final plans to bring Orris down."

I nodded. Peter stepped forward and took Laurus from my arms, and we traveled as a group to the bedroom the omega had been left to recover in. Emery, Vivian, Nana, and the children all had to be back in Eureka Springs, safe and separate from the chaos that was our lives, so there'd been no one to tend to the omega while I shared our story. The room was quiet.

I approached the side of the bed and took the omega's hand. He looked peaceful while in stasis, and I was reluctant to heal him and force him back into the cruel reality of the world, but my king's orders were absolute, and I knew that I had to try, no matter how I felt about it.

I summoned a claw and pricked his skin, drawing a tiny bead of blood. The others entered the room behind me, filling the room and looking over my shoulder. I dipped my finger in the blood, then held it to my tongue and mapped out the pain in his body, just like I always did. Physically, he didn't seem harmed, but there were psychological scars in him that were affecting the composition of his blood. I targeted that darkness, chipping away at it slowly to lessen his tremendous burden.

"He's cold," I murmured. "Brick, can you please bring me a blanket?"

"Of course."

Brick was a gentle giant. With silver streaking his hair and a kind, albeit sometimes stoic face, he reminded me of a father. It was a shame that he'd never had a child—I imagined that little one would never want for love.

He brought a blanket to the bedside and tucked the omega in, but as he did, the darkness in the omega's mind exploded into fragments, and the pain he'd suffered was instantly cured. I gasped and dropped his hand, opening my eyes.

The omega had woken up.

He fluttered his eyes open, confusion plain on his face. He looked up at us, then met Brick's gaze. His smile grew.

"So that's what the heartsong sounds like," the little omega in the bed said. "I thought I'd never hear it... but here you are."

None of us knew what to say, but out of all of us, Brick was the most surprised. Then, to my amazement, he laughed. Tears beaded in his eyes, and he dropped to the side of the bed and took the omega's hand in his own. I knew how he felt —my own heartsong stood not all that far behind me, and his presence still warmed my soul and made me feel complete. It filled me with joy to see that the last of my unmated brothers-at-arms had found his chance at happiness.

There were still dark days to come, their outcome uncertain, but in this moment of wonder, I knew one thing for certain— our lives would never cease to be interesting. At least, not as long as we stuck together... and as long as Peter intended to remain here, I was planning to stay. These men were my friends and my family, and nothing would ever make me want to stray.

SNEAK PEEK AT ALPHA DECEIVED

Need more? Pick up the next Waking the Dragons book, Alpha Victorious, now! Warning: if you're not into daddy alphas who know how to keep their boys in line; cute, but feisty omegas with surprising pasts; in-laws who'll have you rolling on the floor laughing; and a romance that transcends race, this might not be the book for you...

Check out the first chapter on the next page.

1

NATHAN

I was only vaguely aware of the people surrounding me in this strange room—all of my focus was spared for... *him*. I could hear his heartsong as clearly as if it were pounding within my own ears, its special rhythm beating only for me.

Sure, there were other alphas in the world with heartsongs that would have come close enough to match mine, and I probably would have been happy with any of them, but this was different. I knew it from the second I heard it. None other would compare to the perfect way that his matched to mine.

I was too shy to look him directly in the eyes; instead, I gazed up from under my lashes and observed the different parts that made him up. Only briefly did I allow myself to drink in his blue eyes with their silver striations. They matched the silver streaks in his hair and whiskers. I liked that he was older than me. It made me feel safe—like I'd finally found someone who I could trust with anything.

I took in his olive-toned skin and noted the deep wrinkles around his eyes, the kind of lines that only came from a life-time of laughter. He had a strong nose, though slightly bent at the top, as if it had been broken at some point in his life and had never set right. Under a trim, neat mustache lay a pair of almost soft-looking lips—lips that I wanted to feel against my own.

I couldn't help myself. He was a treat for the eyes, and I was starved for him. My tongue ran across my lower lip, and as soon as it did, the man in front of me sucked in a raspy breath and barked out a terse command.

"Out! All of you, wretches. Close the door behind you, and leave me to my heartsong."

My hand wrenched free of his grasp when I reflexively curled up into a protective ball, lying on my side while touching my forehead to my knees. I shook with fear. Shame washed through me, and I found it hard to breathe. Why now, of all times? I'd just found someone I felt I could trust, but here I was, shutting down.

"Dude, he's having a panic attack. I don't think we should leave him if he's freaking out," a hesitant voice said from somewhere near the open door.

"Brick, you're scaring your omega. Take a second and calm down. I know you didn't mean to be so abrupt, but he's been through pain and trauma, and it's made him sensitive. You need to be gentle and take care with him," the man who'd been at my other side when I'd awakened said in a low voice.

Brick. That was the name of my heartsong. It suited him, somehow. His body looked hard as cement, that was for certain. His large hand rested gently in my too-curly hair, his fingers threading through my locks while his thumb stroked back and forth over my forehead.

Instantly, I was able to breathe. His touch centered me and gave me the strength to relax. As I slowly unfurled and straightened into a seated position, his hand went along with my head, carefully moving with me. I was completely naked, I realized as I tried to sit up. I made sure to keep the blankets pooled around my waist, embarrassed.

In a quieter tone, Brick spoke again. "Forgive me, heartsong. I never meant to frighten you, only to make these Nosy Nellies take their leave."

He paused, then spoke more firmly. "In case you all missed it, that's your cue to leave. My heartsong will never be safer anywhere on Earth than he is with me—a fact that you all know. So bugger off and go do what we always do when our friends are busy meeting their mates for the first time—gossip about us and place your wagers on how much sleep I'll be getting. But do it from the other side of the closed door. I want to be alone with—"

He stopped and moved his hand down to tip my chin up, forcing me to make eye contact. "What is your name, dear one? As you've no doubt gathered, I am Brick."

"N-Nathan," I whispered. "But my friends used to call me Nate."

The other man, the one who'd been attending me when I'd awoken, spoke up. "Before I leave, I want to introduce myself. My name is Sana. I am the healer here, and a longtime friend of Brick's. I have just finished examining you, and other than the psychological pain, your body is in good condition."

Sana smiled gently at me before turning his wary gaze to Brick. "Nate needs sustenance. I will return shortly with a tray of food and drink. Do not even think that you'll have your privacy until I'm satisfied that the boy is nourished."

Brick merely raised a brow. "And you honestly believe that my mate's every need is not my utmost concern? I'm disappointed in you, friend. Surely, you know me better than that."

I looked back and forth between the two large, thickly muscled, warrior-looking men like I was a spectator at an awkward tennis match. They spoke over me as if I wasn't sitting right there.

Sana merely rolled his eyes at his friend. He wagged a finger at Brick. "Be that as it may, I can scent the same thing that you can. This boy's heat is approaching. Before your dragon loses himself to lust, let's take the steps to make sure your mate makes it through your breeding session, hmm?"

Before Brick could respond and before I could process the

fact that they were casually discussing my heat, their conversation was thankfully interrupted by a friendly-looking man with hair as blond as my own. He pushed through the crowd in the doorway, holding out a tray.

"Here, Sana. I thought our guest might need some foo—" Before he could finish, he tripped over his own feet and almost crashed down onto the bed with me. A larger man reached out and caught him around the waist with one hand, while another red-haired man caught the tray before it hit the floor.

"Thanks, Cory," the blond said with a grin to the man who'd caught him before turning back to me. The redheaded man handed Brick the tray he'd caught. "Sorry for the dramatic entrance. As I was saying, I thought you might be hungry. I know I would be. Anyway, I'm Emery. It's nice to meet you. Go ahead and shout out if you need anything else. I'll just help these other guys find their way out of here so you can catch your breath and get to know Brick sans audience."

I wasn't sure whether to bless or curse the man as he clapped his hands together and shooed everyone out. On the one hand, my dragon really wanted to be alone with this alpha that sang our heartsong so beautifully. On the other? Holy *shit*. I wasn't at all sure that I was capable of being alone with such a massively sexy creature.

Sana patted my hand one last time and murmured something

to Brick about making sure I ate, then followed the others out into the hall, pulling the door closed behind him. I stared at the closed door, blinking at it as I chewed my lip and wondered what I should do.

I looked up, startled, when Brick's deep voice broke the silence. "Is it okay if I sit beside you, Nathan?"

My mind raced. I wanted him to, but I was unsure how to admit it without sounding desperate. Finally, I nodded and scooted over to make room. Brick smiled, then set the tray on my lap. Its extended legs brought it to just the right height so that it acted like a table.

I sucked in a breath as Brick kicked off his shoes and began stripping off his clothes. What the actual fuck was he doing? He was getting naked? While I ate? Was he trying for solidarity because I was naked, or were his clothes not clean enough for the linens? Surely he wasn't planning to take me while I ate...

My thoughts were intrusive, so I did the only thing I could to settle them—I averted my eyes and stared at the tray in front of me, taking inventory.

The glass of lemonade appeared to hold about sixteen ounces of fluid. There were two sandwiches, cut in half diagonally, with thick slabs of ham and swiss cheese. Blinking, I assessed that each half would take me six bites to eat, so that was twenty-four bites.

To the side was a bowl of cubed cantaloupe. I used the fork to move them around until I counted nine pieces. Nine pieces, but three of them were two-bite chunks, so...

I fell into the security of counting as I added the twelve bites of fruit and the twenty-four bites of sandwich. Thirty-six bites. The lemon bar that sat in the upper-right corner of the tray would easily take four bites. Forty bites total. Good. Even numbers were always good for the digestion.

At twenty chews per bite, it would take—

"What are you thinking about so intensely, Nathan?" Brick asked quietly. At some point during my pre-eating ritual, he'd slid into the bed beside me and was sitting there, his warm skin pressed against my own. One of his arms rested behind me.

Without stopping to think about how Looney Tunes it would sound, I answered him. "Forty bites. This meal will be consumed in forty bites. I can't quantify how many gulps the lemonade will take, because I don't know if it's sweet or sour... but at sixteen ounces, it will likely take seven, although I'll make it eight because odd numbers are unlucky."

I stopped rambling as soon as I realized how ludicrous I must sound. I didn't have a chance to be embarrassed, though.

Brick simply took the fork and speared a piece of fruit. "Then I suggest you begin eating, little one. Here's bite one."

Without hesitation, I opened my lips as the fruit bumped against them. Brick gently positioned it between my teeth, and I bit it from the fork. Silently, I counted my chews while Brick watched. As soon as I'd swallowed, he lifted another piece for me.

We went on like that for several minutes until the fruit was almost done. After I'd taken the ninth bite, Brick's lips pursed thoughtfully, and his brows drew together as he watched while I chewed.

"You're counting your chewing, aren't you? It can't be accidental that every bite takes exactly twenty chews to consume."

My eyes widened in surprise. He'd noticed that? I gulped and reached for the lemonade, forgetting to monitor how much I was taking in as my mind raced. I set it down after draining nearly half the glass.

"Y-you noticed that?" I hated how my voice squeaked when I was nervous. Seriously. At twenty years old, I really should have been past that shit.

"I'm fascinated by you, Nathan. Of course I noticed. Tell me, does this give you peace, or is it something destructive?"

I lifted a shoulder and ignored the offered piece of melon he held out for me. "It gives me peace. I think that's a good description. It's like... the world is scary and way too noisy. It can't be controlled. But I *can* measure and count what I put into my body. My family is loud and crazy, so I'm pretty sure it started when I was little. Although, in my defense, studies have proven that it takes a minimum of twenty chews to properly masticate one's food."

As much as it surprised me that I was so willing to talk to this man, it was also scary to share such a private thing. Brick opened his mouth as if to speak, but I heard footsteps approaching and looked up at the door a second or two before whoever it was knocked.

Brick raised a brow in my direction as he spoke to the door. "This better be important. You may enter."

The awkward one... Emery, I think? He was the one to open the door, and he was followed by the large warrior-like man who'd rescued him from falling.

"I'm sorry to interrupt. I brought more lemonade, and a few bottles of water. Sana felt like dehydration might be a concern for Nate." He smiled and walked over to my side. He set the bottles on my nightstand before turning and tilting the pitcher as if to refill my cup, but Brick held a hand out for the pitcher before he could.

"Thanks, Emery. I'll just take that and top him off when he's ready. This was thoughtful of you—I appreciate the kindness."

Emery smiled and passed Brick the pitcher. He turned to leave, reaching out for the other man's hand, but thought better of it and looked back to me.

"Oh! I almost forgot. You must think I'm rude as heck. This is my mate, Cory. You'll meet everyone later, including our daughter, Cora. She's with her grandma right now, though."

I nodded politely, then froze when Brick spoke softly in my ear. "Cory is our king. I am a warrior sworn to his protection."

Cory rolled his eyes at Brick's words. He gave me a lopsided grin, as if to downplay the statement. "I would be king, if I had a kingdom. Instead, I'm merely a throwback to a world that time has forgotten. Just call me Cory and settle in. I'll let your mate fill you in on our backstory. Hopefully, we will all get an opportunity to know you more come tomorrow. Until then, rest and enjoy this time with your mate."

I bit my lip at his words, dazed by the idea of being in the presence of royalty. All I could do was nod my agreement until I found my voice. "Thank you... both of you. Especially you, Emery. This lemonade is good. Not too sweet or sour, but just right."

Emery grinned proudly, then stepped into the hall while

Cory pulled the door shut after giving Brick a quick wink. I tilted my head and listened to their footsteps fading away before biting half of the melon cube from the fork that had gone back to hovering in front of my mouth.

"I'm guessing that hearing is your superpower, huh?" Brick asked conversationally as I chewed. After I'd swallowed, I nodded.

"Mama Vee says I have ears like a bat, the nerves of a mouse, and the memory of an elephant." I blushed hotly and leaned forward to take the rest of the bite from the fork he held. Brick merely smiled and fed me the rest of the fruit.

He set the fork down when I reached for a sandwich and sat there running an affectionate hand along my back while I ate. I liked that I could be silent with him—he seemed perfectly content with being quiet and wasn't trying to fill every gap with the sound of his own voice. I admired that.

After I'd carefully taken three more gulps of lemonade, draining the glass in four rather than eight, Brick refilled my glass, then set the pitcher on the nightstand next to him.

It meant more than I could ever put into words that he understood that I needed to finish the exact amount I'd planned on drinking before adding any extra.

Halfway through the first sandwich, Brick began telling me a tale of five men frozen in time for ten thousand years while the world had moved on without them.

He spoke quietly, telling me how Cory and his three protectors had been on the run during a civil war between their people, only to be attacked by their own adviser.

In self-defense, Brick had used his nature-bending powers to pull the stone from the mountain cavern where they'd been attacked in order to protect them, encasing them all as their bodies underwent emergency healing stasis.

My mind raced as he told me the latest hardships his group had suffered at the hands of this Orris person—their two-faced adviser. I had just swallowed the last of the delicious lemon bar and was reaching for my glass of lemonade when he dropped the final bomb of the story.

"Orris is the same man that held you captive, Nathan. When you're ready, we'll need to discuss him. I know that my friends are waiting to debrief you, but they've been kind enough to give us this time to become acquainted."

I pulled my hands away from the glass—my hands had begun to shake violently. My breaths came in short, hard pants as memories flashed in and out of my mind, some clearer than others, but none of them good.

"Hey, now. You're safe, little one. I will not ever let him touch you again, trust that." As he spoke, Brick took the tray from my lap and deposited it on the nightstand next to the pitcher. Then, with nothing blocking me from him anymore, he pulled me onto his lap and held me close.

Safety. Compassion. Stability.

I closed my eyes and let him take care of me in all the ways that I could never take care of myself.

**

Click here to pick up your copy of Alpha Victorious, now available on Amazon!

STAY IN TOUCH

What happens when your fated mate is also your natural predator?
Join Susi Hawke's mailing list and get your FREE copy of The Rabbit Chase

Can't get enough omegaverse?
Join Piper Scott's mailing list and get your FREE copy of the oh, so sexy Yes, Professor

Find Susi Hawke on Facebook:
https://www.facebook.com/susihawkeauthor

Find Piper Scott on Facebook:
https://www.facebook.com/groups/PiperScott

Rent-a-Dom Series

(with Piper Scott)

Made in the USA
Las Vegas, NV
23 September 2021

30900145R10157